BACKWATER FLATS

A KURT HUNTER MYSTERY

STEVEN BECKER

Copyright © 2013 by Steven Becker
All rights reserved.
No part of this book may be reproduced in any form or by any electronic or mechanical means, including information storage and retrieval systems, without written permission from the author, except for the use of brief quotations in a book review.

Join my mailing list
and get a free copy of my starter library:
First Bite

Click the image or download here: http://eepurl.com/-obDj

BACKWATER FLATS

1

STEVEN BECKER
A KURT HUNTER MYSTERY
BACKWATER FLATS

The National Park Service, my employer, has a dual mandate: Protect our natural resources while at the same time provide opportunities for public use. Today I was part of the public enjoying Biscayne National Park. I made sure my daughter, Allie, stayed to the posted no-wake speed as she ran my park-service-issue twenty-two-foot center console. She executed a perfect entry into the canal leading to Bayfront.

To the left, across a small lagoon, was a spit of trucked-in sand that made do as a beach here. The iconic white strip of real beach that ran down the east coast of Florida, ended at South Beach, just visible in front of the Miami skyline to the north. A good-weather Sunday drew a large crowd to the park and at the boat ramp. Weekend afternoons the park and canal were a zoo. That often meant problems for agents, but today was my day off. Lining up in the stream of traffic heading back to the boat ramp, I was fortunate our stop was instead the gas dock, allowing us to avoid the true logjam, just a hundred feet farther at the boat ramp.

"Nice and easy. Cut the power and see what the wind and current do," I coached Allie as she approached the dock. If we were going to enter the side channel leading to the park headquarters we would have switched positions. Not because she couldn't handle the traffic, but to avoid my boss, Special Agent in Charge, Martinez, and his slew of surveillance cameras, spotting her driving my boat.

"Dad—"

Yes, my seventeen-year-old could drive a car and run a boat almost as well as I could, but that didn't stop advice from pouring from my mouth. She skillfully read the conditions and coasted up against the rub rail of the fuel dock. Will, the attendant, came over to help with the lines.

"Hey, Allie. Catch anything?" he asked.

He wasn't ignoring me, but rather flirting with my daughter. I let Allie enjoy the accolades. Will was in her age bracket, but she'd shown little interest in him other than as a friend.

"Finally got a cubera." She reached into the cooler, grabbed the fish behind its gill plate, and proudly held up the thirty-inch-long bucktooth snapper.

"Nice one." He came over and fist-bumped her.

Though the boat ramp was bustling with activity, the fuel dock was quiet. One other boat, a trawler, probably a resident of the small marina located just past the ramp, occupied the long dock. With gas at marinas costing at least a dollar more per gallon than at gas stations, most boaters who trailered would fuel up along the way to save some money. Many were unaware of the ethanol they were pouring into their tanks, which was absent in the REC-90 fuel offered at marinas and at just a few gas stations. Although I got my paychecks from the feds, I favored neither political party and thought myself an independent. As I reached over and handed Will my personal credit card to pay for replacing the park service gas that I had used today, I wondered how many of those unknowing boaters voted for the guys who thought that adding ten percent ethanol to regular gas would save the world. To my knowledge, all it accomplished was to subsidize corn production and ruin small engines.

While Will ran the card, I glanced back at a loud noise coming from the direction of the ramp. It was an odd feeling, being both in a pristine wilderness area and this close to a mass of humanity, many of whom were well over the legal limit for alcohol. Living on one of the barrier islands several miles across the bay, I needed little other than groceries from the mainland and, unless I had to, spent my days out on the water—miles from here.

"I gotta go," Allie said, laying the fish on the cooler and pulling a fillet knife from the sheath by the console.

We generally split our catch, but, eyeing the Florida Fish and Wildlife Conservation Commission boat sitting across the canal I thought better of filleting it onboard. The laws were clear that fish needed to be whole until brought ashore. My boss, Martinez, would have been delighted in my misfortune if I was cited.

"Take it, I have plenty," I told her.

"You sure? Mom'll be blown away. She usually just sees the fillets."

"No worries. But I wish I could enjoy it with you," I said, feeling guilty the minute the words were out of my mouth. Allie lived with her mom during the week. It was a suitable custody arrangement that only had to last for another school year. I would have liked more time with her, but recognized her need for a stable home—one on the mainland, closer to civilization.

Holding the fish under the gills, she stepped onto the dock and waved. Watching her walk away, I had a small anxiety attack as she opened the driver-side door of the Honda sedan and slid behind the wheel. The car started and I heard the bass booming from the speakers as she pulled away. It was a new thing, driving herself between Palm Beach, where her mom lived, and Homestead, where the marina was, something I wasn't entirely comfortable with. It wasn't her inexperience—she was a good driver—but rather the ninety miles of South Florida craziness separating her parents.

I stood there until she was out of sight, then turned to watch the activity at the park ramp. All sorts of mayhem was ensuing as a steady stream of boats were being pulled from the water. I'd often thought municipalities could increase their revenue by adding bleachers and charging admission to their ramps. There are some things few people are good at, and one of those is trailering a boat. Done on your own, with no one watching, it's not difficult to splash and retrieve a vessel. On busy days like this, when there was a line of boats in the water and trucks jockeying for position on land, it was like a trash can waiting for a match. Fueled by alcohol, it brought out the worst in people.

I watched several bungled attempts by one couple until a blinding light caught my attention. Across the water, the FWC boat's light bar flashed as it pulled over one of the incoming boats. I'd seen this show before. Instead of patrolling the waters looking for infractions, they set up what amounted to a roadblock in the canal just before the ramp, checking every sixth or seventh boat. I'd heard grumblings about the officers issuing safety citations, as well as confiscating shorts. "Not my department" was my general opinion, and I did my best to get along with the officers—except for Pete Robinson, the head of the local team. I'd found him to be on par with my boss, Martinez.

Checking my phone, I sat on the leaning post and with a half-hour to kill until my wife, Justine arrived, I watched the show. While I waited, I observed several marital disputes, one altercation that a pair of county officers fortunately were on-hand for, and one truck that slid door-deep into the water. Across the channel, the FWC officers were busy harassing the fishermen and had pulled over no less than four boats.

"Hey, what'cha thinkin' about?"

Realizing I was more interested in the drama around me than I thought, I turned and smiled, seeing Justine standing on the dock. My wife of half-a-dozen months, her arms laden with grocery bags, and with the sweetest smile I could ever hope for, leaned in and handed me several of the bags.

"Permission to come aboard?"

"Anytime." I took the groceries, set them on the deck, and though she didn't need it, I offered a hand. She launched herself into my arms and we held a long, passionate kiss.

"Allie got her cubera! Saw a post on Instagram," Justine said.

I was proud enough of my daughter to ignore the fact that she must have posted it while driving, and Justine must have seen it while she was on the road, too. When that dawned on me, I promised myself to bring it up later—with both of them.

"Didn't want any problem with the officers." I nodded my head in the direction of the FWC boat across the way. "So I gave her the whole fish."

"Your ex is going to love that."

I hadn't thought about Jane not knowing what to do with a whole fish, and the cubera snapper with its two fangs was frightening-looking. I smiled, taking a small pleasure in her discomfort.

"You ready? No worries on the fish. I got some nice steaks for dinner," Justine said.

"You bet." Anticipating a red-meat dinner, I turned to the wheel while she freed the lines. Living on the water, we had fresh fish most nights. I avoided the boat ride to my truck on the mainland and the subsequent drive to the grocery store like the plague. As a result, we rarely had meat.

I glanced across the canal once more, seeing the officers pick a new victim from the stream of incoming boats. I used the gap created by the detained boat to back into the canal, letting the boat turn around before pushing the throttle forward. Obeying the no-wake speed limit, I idled toward the markers leading toward open water and my island.

Adams Key, six miles to the southeast, was my government-issued home. From the mainland, the island was a small blur on the horizon—on a good day. Although it grew in size as we approached, at only a few acres and with only two homes, the island never seemed large. Most days there was a certain romance associated with living on an island this far from the mainland. This was not one of those days. Caesar Creek, one of the few well-marked passes connecting Biscayne Bay to the Atlantic, lay alongside Adams Key and had a continuous stream of boats passing through. Each one threw its wake against the long concrete dock that serviced our island. It was mostly empty, used only by my neighbor Ray, me, and a few park visitors to a little-known day-use area.

The water was disturbed enough that I had to wait for a suitable gap between the boat wakes before I could dock. When I did, I heard Zero's toenails click as he rumbled down the concrete dock and skidded to a stop. The greeting was not for me. Zero, Ray and Becky's pit bull mix that reminded me of Petey from the Little Rascals, and I were buddies, but his real love interest was Justine. Hopping onto the dock, she squatted down to his eye level and rubbed his jowls.

While they communed, I carried the groceries and her backpack up the stairs of my stilt house. Setting the bags on the counter in the kitchen I went back to retrieve my wife, but it was too late.

"Nice work. Justine said you got Allie on a cubera." A cold beer extended from Ray's hand, which, although I had other activities in mind, I reluctantly accepted. Their toddler, Jamie, was now garnering Justine's attention. With two hands holding her very pregnant belly, Becky came over to greet me. We chatted for a bit until Ray got tired of the girls' talk and retreated back to their house. Zero remained undecided when Becky took Jamie back home, eventually following Justine upstairs to our house. With a loud moan, and an eye on the grocery bags, he crashed to the cool tile floor in the kitchen.

Zero had a longer wait than he might have wanted. Once the door was closed, I grabbed Justine and headed for the bedroom. Though we'd been married almost six months, the logistics of our jobs required us to be apart several days a week. Justine was a forensics tech for Miami-Dade and still kept her old condo in Miami. With the run across the bay it was a too-lengthy, unreliable, and complicated commute to try on a daily basis.

"Go on and light the grill. I'll get the steaks ready," Justine said a half-hour later, almost tripping over a snoring Zero still crashed in the middle of the floor.

Just as I stepped onto the porch and lifted the grill's cover, I heard the distinctive Darth Vader ringtone from my work phone. Martinez calling on a Sunday night was a very unusual occurrence. Reaching the counter just as it stopped ringing, I waited for the inevitable voicemail. The ding came seconds later and I put the phone on speaker so Justine could hear the call. If it was what I suspected, she would be involved as well.

"Hunter. We've got a body."

2

STEVEN BECKER
A KURT HUNTER MYSTERY
BACKWATER FLATS

We both stared at the phone, listening to Martinez command my presence at the crime scene. His order meant something different to each of us. Justine's face showed her excitement; mine was a more pensive look. Not that her job was easy, but it had defined lines. The Park Service's limited budget, controlled to the penny by Martinez, didn't allow for the infrastructure to work crimes in-house. We were beholden to Miami-Dade or the Florida Department of Law Enforcement for support. My preference was the FDLE, but with their closest lab five hours away in Tampa, it wasn't a practical option. Instead, I was saddled with the bureaucracy and politics of Miami's finest. The bright spot in the quagmire was Justine. She would check and evaluate the crime scene, then process the evidence. The only pressure was to not make a mistake that would render a crucial piece of evidence inadmissible, and affect a trial. As one of two special agents assigned to the park, the lines on both my jurisdiction and my ability to work crimes were vague.

Jurisdiction was an issue. With only a handful of permanent residents, crimes committed inside the park rarely ended there. The 270- square miles that made up the park were ninety-five percent water, leaving my landlubbing boss restricted to the remaining five percent. The other special agent, my oftentimes nemesis, Susan McLeash, preferred her air-conditioned office to the waterways, leaving me free to roam the top of the Florida Keys ecosystem alone. Geologically, the Keys start with the northernmost boundary islands in the park, well northeast of Key Largo, and end seventy miles beyond Key West in the Dry Tortugas. With over two-hundred islands extending over that many miles, there are plenty of places for both recreation and nefarious activity. It's easy to get lost in the maze of islands, and the Keys reputation as a smuggler's paradise remains intact.

"He did say the body was found near headquarters, didn't he?" I asked. Justine nodded, but I pressed the button to repeat the voicemail just in case.

"Guess the steaks are going to have to wait," Justine said, as she returned to the bedroom to put on something more appropriate.

"Glad we had date night already." Thankful for our earlier rendezvous, I followed her in and changed into my uniform. "You think we might stay at your place tonight?"

"If the body is on the mainland, it might make sense," she said, repacking the few items she had brought in her backpack.

We both had full wardrobes and personal items here and at her condo, but there was always something to be dragged back and forth. Removing my gun belt from the hook placed high enough in the closet to keep the weapon out of reach in case Jamie visited, I slung it around my waist, fastened the buckle, and took one last look around. After replacing the steaks in the refrigerator and turning off the grill, we were followed down the stairs by a disgruntled Zero. Sensing his night out was over, Zero parted ways with us where the walk split, ambled up to the stairs at Ray's house—a mirror image of ours—where he stopped and barked. The screen door opened and he waddled up the stairs without casting a look back.

Riding across the bay into the setting sun would have been enjoyable except for what awaited us on the mainland—Martinez wouldn't have called if this was as simple as a natural death. The boat traffic continued to be heavy as we entered the channel, and I fought to restrain myself and stay in line. After almost two years in the park I knew which markers were surrounded by deep enough water that I could cut inside, but knowing the recreational boaters would see me and then think it was okay, I stayed within the lines.

Passing the ramp, I noticed the FWC boat was gone, allowing the boaters one less thing to worry about as they left the water. I turned to the right and entered the small marina in back of the headquarters building. Pushing my boat envy aside, I passed a Johnny Wells quad-powered 39' Interceptor and then the FWC, twin-engine, rigid-hull inflatable boat. I pulled into the slip reserved for my more modest single-engine center console and killed the power.

There were no first responders in sight as we walked down the dock, and I held onto the hope that whatever had happened had occurred just another hundred yards past the docks, outside of the park's boundaries. Soon it was clear that wasn't the case. Rounding the building, we saw an ambulance and several Miami-Dade cruisers in the parking lot. Crime-scene tape was already strung across several parking spaces. As we approached I was relieved when I didn't recognize either of the officers—I had few allies in the Miami-Dade ranks.

Introducing myself, I lifted the yellow tape and scanned the scene. A small river of blood led me around the FWC truck to a body. Prone on the ground was one of the officers who had been working the channel earlier. Turning back to see where Justine was, I noticed her talking on her cell, probably getting approval to work the scene. There are steps and procedures for a death, starting with the Medical Examiner's arrival. It was no surprise when I heard the squeal of rubber against the hot asphalt. Usually working an active crime scene is a hurry-up-and-wait affair, but not today. The Miami-Dade Medical Examiner's van sped straight toward us. Hunched over the wheel with his head almost pressing against the windshield, Sid flew across the lot and screeched to a stop just outside the taped-off perimeter. The door opened and the older man stepped out onto the hot asphalt. Working the kinks out of his back, he hobbled over to me.

"Hunter, you're a shit magnet," he said. His gaze shifted past me and, ignoring my outstretched hand, he hugged Justine. Finally, he returned his attention to me.

"I didn't find this one," I said, trying not to sound too defensive. During my first few months here I had found several bodies while fishing. The reputation still haunted me.

He shook his head and approached the body. Taking a pair of gloves from his pocket, he snapped them on and, in what appeared to be a painful movement, bent down and checked the man's carotid artery. There was little doubt the officer was dead, but procedures had to be followed. Now that Sid was here, the investigation could proceed.

In front of us was a chain-link security fence that bordered the Park Service parking lot. On the other side was Miami-Dade County. Even though we were only a car's length away from city territory, the body had landed inside the park. Walking to the two officers, I handed them my card and introduced myself, explaining that as we were inside the park boundary, I would be taking the case. They seemed relieved, gave me a brief summary of the call they received and the actions they had taken, and were quickly on their way.

Turning back to Sid, I watched as he photographed the body

from twenty-seven angles, then, with Justine's help, rolled the deceased onto his back. Our eyes all went to the blood-stained front of his uniform shirt.

"Knife wound." Sid started talking, as Justine recorded the details. "Just under the sternum. Must have died quickly."

I removed my own notebook and pen, and started writing down the specifics. Looking at the deceased, I realized he must have been off-duty and wasn't wearing the bulletproof vest that probably would have saved his life. Time of death wasn't a question. I had seen the officer alive not two hours ago. Because the heat coming off the parking lot, I doubted that, unless there was some other clue, Sid would calculate a time of death any closer.

"I saw him working the channel about two hours ago," I said.

"Seems about right." Sid looked up.

"We were out at Adams for an hour or so." I looked down at the time stamp on Martinez's message on my phone. "Call came in at 4:30. I'd say he was killed around 4:00."

"And that's why you're the detective."

His sarcasm was interrupted by a man walking toward us. I expected that word would have gotten out about the fallen officer, but seeing Pete Robinson this quickly, and on a Sunday was unusual.

"Hunter," the FWC supervisor greeted me.

Bucking the trend for guys with male-pattern baldness to shave their heads, the outline of Robinson's receding hairline was clearly evident. It was Sunday and I hadn't expected him to be in uniform, but after inspecting his neatly pressed Hawaiian shirt, I had to wonder where he had come from. The large flower print did nothing to conceal his girth.

"Robinson." I returned the greeting. "Sorry for your loss."

"Hayward was a fine officer." He shook his head.

I doubted I would get much more from the elusive Pete Robinson. Sharing the marina as we did, most of the officers and

I were on a first-name basis. Their boss was seldom seen anywhere near the water, often leading me to wonder if he was Martinez's golf partner.

"I saw him working the channel with another officer earlier this afternoon. Any idea who that was?"

"Have to check the schedule. I'll get back to you on that." He walked around the truck as if he was looking for something, then returned to the body.

"Wife? Next of kin?" I called out as he opened the truck door.

"I'll send over a copy of his file."

I almost told him not to bother, but I didn't expect that he would go out of his way to do so, and I wondered again why he had come by. My questions would have gone unanswered anyway, as the truck sped out of the lot faster than a spooked bonefish. Sid had a body bag on the ground next to the man and looked like he was about to wrap up this stage of his investigation. Before I could offer to help, he and Justine rolled the man into the outstretched bag and closed the zipper. Sid rose slowly, placing his hands behind his back and stretching, before moving toward the van.

"A hand, Hunter?" he called out as he opened the rear doors.

Together we pulled the gurney out, dropped the wheels, and moved it next to the body bag. A minute later the wheels screeched again as the van pulled away. He hadn't mentioned an autopsy, but I was sure I'd be getting an invitation. In addition to the opportunity to spend time with Justine, whom he treated like a favorite child, he liked nothing better than to watch me turn green.

Justine walked over to her car and returned with two cases of equipment. I hesitated to interfere, knowing any offer to help would be declined. She was systematic and thorough. Unless forced to, she insisted on working her scenes solo. "I'm going to see if anyone is at the marina, then get online and find the next of kin. I don't want to wait for Robinson."

Now in her zone, she barely nodded as I walked away. As I expected, the marina was quiet. Susan McLeash's boat, identical to mine, was tied down as if expecting a hurricane. A light coating of pollen and dirt told me she hadn't left the comfort of her office lately. Walking by a pole that held one of Martinez's security cameras, I was tempted to wave, but passed by with my head down.

Near the ICE Interceptor and the FWC twin-engine RHIB I had passed earlier, two other boats with FWC decals were docked. The RHIB was FWC's Robinson's rarely used "personal" vessel. The two docked boats were simple, single-engine center consoles similar to mine. The farthest from me glistened with a sheen of water, as if it had recently been hosed down.

Approaching the still-damp boat, I wondered if I should bring it to Justine's attention, but the victim clearly had been murdered in the parking lot. There might be evidence of some kind aboard, but it wasn't the crime scene. Checking my boat shoes to make sure there was no oil or contaminants clinging to them from the parking lot, I stepped across the two feet of water between the dock and the boat.

Checking the helm, I saw no personal items left behind. Next, I opened the hatch and inspected the console, finding mostly safety gear, and again I could see nothing that would reveal anything about the two officers who had used the boat earlier. There were several other holds; one contained a coiled line, another held two fenders. Suspecting this boat held no secrets, I approached the built-in cooler in front of the console and opened the lid. I expected nothing, but found it partially full of ice.

That was interesting. Rather than having to clean this large cooler after a shift, most agents, including myself, brought our own personal coolers aboard. Leaning over, I could see from the way the leftover ice cubes bonded together that someone had hosed it down, which you might do if it had been used for fish. Several small, orange-and-black-colored flakes adhered to the ice and I leaned over to inspect them. I knew from the color and texture that they were swimmerets from the tail section of the locally harvested spiny lobsters— something I hadn't expected to see.

3

STEVEN BECKER
A KURT HUNTER MYSTERY
BACKWATER FLATS

As the sun set, and twilight disappeared, darkness encompassed the site, making it difficult for Justine to work. I'd been back and forth between the FWC boat, first to grab a few evidence bags, then taking some pictures of the cooler in the process. I received a skeptical look from Justine when I showed her the contents.

"Pleopods? Really? Thinking those are the murder weapon, Detective?"

I was dutifully embarrassed, first that I didn't know their proper name, and second that Justine did. She surely had studied anatomy, but I would have thought it was of the human species, not spiny lobsters, which, she previously had informed me, were actually crawfish. I was also informed that all decapods have pleopods. Insisting that these might mean something to the investigation, I added them to the growing pile of evidence bags.

"I'll go look for some lights." I started to the headquarters building, knowing Justine clearly was committed to wrapping up the scene in the dark.

"That'd be good. Maybe you could spin your truck around and point the headlights this way first."

I did as she asked, then headed for the building. Unlocking the door, I smiled for Martinez's camera, mounted not-so-discreetly behind the receptionist's, Mariposa's, desk and headed upstairs. Susan McLeash's and Martinez's offices had views of the marina; mine had no windows. Pushing the unlocked door open, I turned on the light and plopped down in my chair. The aged computer took its time booting up and while I waited I pulled out a legal pad and started making some notes.

Solving a murder was much the same as solving a jigsaw puzzle. First you need the "corners," which I made separate columns for: MOTIVE, MEANS, OPPORTUNITY, and TRIGGER. I had no idea of the motive yet, so I left that space blank, and moved on to the opportunity column, where I wrote "schedule." Unless the dead officer was being followed, which was unlikely seeing as he had spent his day on the water, the killer knew in advance where and when to find their victim—in the parking lot at the end of a shift.

Next, I thought about the means. Justine might find some evidence—hopefully the murder weapon—though I doubted it. Sid had indicated it was a knife wound, but the killer easily could have taken the weapon with him, or tossed it into the canal that ran behind the parking lot. I hoped Sid would be able to specify the size and type of blade when he did his autopsy. The examination would also reveal if there had been a struggle. In either case, I was of the opinion that the killer and victim had known each other.

The last column, labeled trigger, meant whatever event had caused the perpetrator to kill. The difference between manslaughter and murder is premeditation. I would need to figure out if this was a cold-blooded, planned killing, or an emotional reaction. In either case, I had to find why it happened.

Staring at the mostly blank paper, determining Hayward's schedule was the logical starting point. I made a note to find out how many people knew the victim would be in the parking lot at that time. Pete Robinson had promised his personnel file and, with nothing better to do while I waited for Justine, I brought up his contact information on my phone and pressed connect. Since he'd never directly answered my calls before, and expecting his voicemail to pick up, I started composing a message in my head when he answered: "Hunter."

"Sorry to bother you, but I was wondering who has access to agents' schedules?"

There was a pause and I wondered if he had really intended to accept the call or had made a mistake. "I make them, but all the agents can see them. A few other admin folks probably, and that's about it."

Along with most other government agencies, I assumed the FWC had budget restraints as well. "How many agents are in this area?"

"This office covers Palm Beach to Key West. There are eight agents and four admins."

"Any chance I can get names and contact info?"

He reluctantly agreed to give me the information, along with Hayward's personnel file, in the morning. I thanked him and disconnected.

Just as I put the phone down, it rang. Sid's name showed in the display and I answered.

"Agent Hunter. You and your lovely wife are invited to the autopsy, which will begin precisely at eleven tonight."

I knew Justine would be thrilled, and since she was used to working the swing shift at the lab, the late hour wouldn't bother her. I was already tired—and hungry—something I would have to think carefully about with the pending autopsy. Since there was no way out of it, I accepted.

His job as the night and weekend Medical Examiner was Sid's "retirement." He could have run the department, but had chosen to work the "quieter" hours. Sid had a good relationship with his boss, the much younger and hipper Vance Able, who he had chosen to mentor. With decades of experience, Sid generally made short work of the procedure, something I was always grateful for.

Leaving the office I walked downstairs, waved at the camera, and locked the door behind me. Across the dark parking lot I found Justine on her hands and knees near the blood-stained asphalt. That meant she was close to finished. I'd seen her work crime scenes often enough to know that she started at the perimeter and worked her way in to the center, so as not to cross over her work, or to contaminate any evidence.

"Almost done." She scraped a sample of the partially congealed blood into a bag and stood up.

"Sid is doing the autopsy at eleven. I'm assuming you're interested."

"Duh."

I often wondered if Justine found dead bodies more interesting than live ones. "Suppose you want to eat first?" I hoped the answer would be no, but I wasn't surprised when she said yes. Staying outside the yellow tape, I helped load the packed cases in her car and we agreed on a restaurant. Following her back to the turnpike, I started to think about the information. Robinson had been surprisingly cooperative for someone who had barely acknowledged me over the past two years. Sure, one of his agents had been killed, but a personal appearance on a Sunday afternoon was out of character.

My mind drifted back to the cooler on the boat and the fact that, apparently, lobsters had been kept on ice. It occurred to me they must have been the shorts confiscated by the agents. That made sense, but I wondered what had happened to them. It was unlikely that anyone coming into Bayfront Park on a Sunday afternoon would bring evidence of poaching aboard their boats, intentional or not. Most divers and fishermen, knowing the consequences were steep, were conscientious about measuring their catches. In fact, it was illegal to be in the water in pursuit of lobster without a gauge to measure them.

Still, some did, maybe hoping the carapace, the hard section of shell starting between the eyes and extending to the beginning of the tail section, might grow on the way in, or was close enough to the mandated three inches they didn't care and thought no one else would, either. As the activity on the water near the ramp showed earlier, that assumption could land a hefty fine. Measuring was a simple and clear-cut procedure. After hooking one end of the gauge between the eyes, if the other end failed to hit the hard carapace and instead fell to the softer tail section, it was a short. If it landed on the hard shell, it was a keeper.

I made a mental note to ask Robinson about the disposition of the confiscated lobsters and fish when I talked to him tomorrow. By the time I had thought through everything, we had arrived at the restaurant, a family-owned Mexican place on the Miami River. Parking next to Justine, I previewed the menu in my head, deciding that plain chips and maybe some rice were probably going to be my best bet. We were greeted by the hostess and seated outside on a narrow deck.

"Still don't trust yourself?" Justine asked, after I had ordered a ginger ale and Spanish rice for dinner.

"That old man's just waiting for me to lose my lunch on the floor."

"Probably, and this autopsy might be a juicy one."

I pushed the basket of chips away. My first few dead bodies

had been floaters. After a body has been in the water for any length of time, the gore factor is reduced. I'd viewed a few fresh ones lately, but, remembering the blood stain on the front of Hayward's shirt, I had an idea this was going to be ugly. While Justine finished her burrito, and I picked at my rice, I reviewed my list of excuses to leave the autopsy.

Sid greeted us at the side door of the Medical Examiner's office and led us down the hallway to the exam room. Laid out on the table was Agent Hayward, now stripped of his uniform. I was surprised there was not much blood, but I was still glad for my dinner choice. My aversion to autopsies was more influenced by the setting, than of the condition of the deceased. The sterile tile floor, stainless-steel tables, and fluorescent lights seemed to exacerbate the antiseptic smell. Donning a gown, mask, and goggles, and clenching my gut, I followed Sid and Justine into the room.

The procedure went surprisingly quickly. Saltwater had erased much of the evidence on my prior cases, making it a lengthier process to find the cause of death. This time, though Sid was thorough, it was clearly evident what had killed Hayward.

When he was finished with the weighing, measuring, and inspection of the corpse and its components, Sid then focused on the wound. There was no evidence of a struggle, confirming my theory that Hayward knew the killer well enough to allow him to approach. At this point I was assuming it was a man, but a strong woman could easily have done this. Prodding the wound with various implements, Sid determined the murder weapon was somewhere between a four-to-six-inch knife with a serrated edge. My first thought was a bait knife, common to just about every fisherman, a category in which Hayward was sure to have made some enemies.

The procedure complete, I helped Sid replace the corpse in

the bag and wheel it to an empty compartment in the refrigerated wall.

"I'm proud of you." Justine punched my arm as we exited the room and stripped off the protective gear. "That was your first start-to-finish. Somehow, you've always found an excuse to get out of the gory part."

I hadn't realized it, but she was right, and now I was famished. "Do we have any food at home?"

"I'm sure I can find something." She winked.

We thanked Sid, who sat behind his desk pecking with two fingers at the keyboard. He waved us off, and we left through the side door. I was surprised when I looked to the east and saw a faint pink line on the horizon. Checking my phone, I realized it was almost dawn.

"Were you planning on paddling this morning?" I asked Justine.

"Sure. I don't have to be at work until two. Got plenty of time for a nap."

We were on Justine-time, but knowing there would be a summons from Martinez in a few hours, I expected there was no sleep coming my way. "Mind if I tag along?"

"Cool. Interval day. Better get something in your stomach."

Justine was an accomplished stand-up paddleboard racer. I had started to practice with her and had even attempted a race, which was cut short by a drifting boat and a body. I reached for her hand and pulled her against me. "See ya there." I kissed her.

We went to our separate vehicles and a few minutes later were at the condo. After downing a quick smoothie, we loaded the boards and, just as the sun was starting to lighten the sky, headed to the beach. Crossing the Rickenbacker Causeway I could see a light chop on the water.

"Think there's any bumps?" I asked her. Though I was just learning, I was really enjoying catching what waves I could.

"Intervals today. The plan remains the plan."

My idea shot down, we parked on the bay side and unloaded the boards. The exercise felt good, clearing my mind and releasing the tenseness in my body. That is, until we started the first set and the gap between us opened. Pulling as hard as I could, I closed it near the end of the last minute of the interval, but Justine kept a commanding lead. As she looked back at me, illuminated by the sun, her smile made losing acceptable.

Her interval workouts were intense, but typically short, and an hour later we were heading back to the condo. I couldn't help but notice the tension and anxiety starting to creep in on me as the clock ticked toward my inevitable meeting with Martinez.

4

STEVEN BECKER
A KURT HUNTER MYSTERY
BACKWATER FLATS

One of the benefits of being slower than Justine was watching her from behind. After an hour of that view I was ready to take the lead as we entered the condo. True to form, Martinez called just as the door closed, putting an end to any extracurricular activities I had in mind.

Leaving Justine to her morning nap, I left for headquarters. Monday morning traffic became my first obstacle, as brake lights from the road ahead were visible before I exited the parking lot. Road construction raced to stay ahead of the increasing population but, despite the near-constant disruptions, the streets rarely seemed to improve. I'd left about twice the time needed so, as unwelcome as the delay was, I would make my meeting. Sacrificing my coffee stop as a bit of insurance, I rubbed my eyes and waited for the traffic to start moving.

Finally, after turning south on the turnpike I caught a break that put me at the headquarters parking lot entrance about fifteen minutes early. Pulling in, I noticed the crime-scene tape was still in place. A small group of Park Service personnel and FWC officers stood, heads bowed, outside the perimeter. To my surprise, Susan McLeash was one of them.

Parking in my usual spot, I climbed out of the truck and headed over to the group.

"Heard you caught the case," Susan said. Her tone was harsh.

I'd hoped the impromptu memorial would stifle her bitterness, but it persisted. Sidled up against one of the FWC officers, Hayward's partner (if memory served from observing them yesterday), she either knew the man or was angling for a date. There was no attempt at respect for the dead in her wardrobe and makeup. With her uniform just a little too tight in all the wrong places and wearing enough makeup that I worried it would crack if she showed any emotion, Susan looked decidedly out of place among the somber group.

Checking my phone, I saw I still had ten minutes until my meeting with Martinez and stuck around the outskirts of the mourners, hoping they might break up and I could speak to Hayward's partner. Just as I was about to leave, the group broke up. I moved closer to Susan, taking a deep breath as I approached to avoid at least that first waft of her heavy perfume. As she chatted up the FWC officer, I could see he didn't mind the stench. From the look of him, the department didn't require physicals and, in his world, Susan might be a catch. I tried to use that to my advantage.

"Who's your friend, Susan?"

"Jim Scott," he said as he extended his hand.

I studied the man for a brief second. Curiosity got the better of me after seeing the way Susan was stalking him. I couldn't help but check out his ring finger, not surprised to find a wide, gold band ensconced on the pudgy digit. From the look of it, cutting it off would be the only method to remove it. That indicated he had been married when he was a thinner, and probably younger, man. Susan apparently didn't care.

"You were on duty with Officer Hayward yesterday? I saw you out in the channel."

"Right, he was my partner." He turned back, glancing down at the dried blood staining the parking lot.

"I'm Kurt Hunter, a special agent here. I've been assigned the case." I reached into my pocket and pulled out a card, which I handed to him. "Do you have any time we can talk? I've got to go into a meeting with my boss now." I didn't expect it to last long —they never did.

"Robinson's got me scheduled this morning. I could meet you this afternoon."

I wondered why a supervisor wouldn't give a deceased man's partner a break, but then I wouldn't expect Martinez to have extended me any courtesies in the same circumstances, either. We set a time and I started toward the main entrance.

Mariposa was always a welcome sight. Sitting behind the reception desk, she smiled and with her Caribbean lilt asked about Allie and Justine. I told her they were fine and inquired about her husband, trying to snag another invitation to dinner with them—and her husband's Appleton 21, his "guest-only" rum. She waved me off, telling me with her expression that the boss was waiting.

Climbing the stairs, I wondered how Martinez was going to handle this. Interagency investigations were always difficult, with each organization trying to protect their turf. Having Martinez and Robinson heading the local offices was not going to make it any easier. My only hope was the constant hammering about his budget would be set aside as the FWC would offset the cost of the investigation.

I was right on one count and wrong on the other. The only surprise was that the chair next to mine, often occupied by Susan McLeash, was empty. That was good news. At least for now I would be free of my permanent nemesis and occasional partner. Martinez's eyes remained glued to the three monitors on his desk when I entered. My greeting was a wave of his hand.

"Distracting having a crime scene in our parking lot," I said, in an attempt to get the meeting going.

I could see around the edge of his monitor that he was watching the lot. I leaned forward. "Do you have footage from yesterday?" Reluctantly, as if he was giving up state secrets, he shifted the monitor toward me and with the mouse panned the view across the lot. I inferred from the display that the camera had been pointed elsewhere yesterday.

"Any footage would help." Maybe I would catch a break and see the perpetrator enter or leave the area.

"I'll be reviewing it." He looked at me as if I was the guilty party.

I felt my face flush at the comment. The time stamp on the video would vindicate me. His snarky tone rattled me and I breathed in, trying not to show it. "Good thing Justine was there. We got the scene processed last night. I met the Medical Examiner on-site and attended the autopsy last night." I yawned for effect.

If I expected an "attaboy" it never came. "I may need a hand with Pete Robinson," I said.

"I'm thinking about passing this off to Miami-Dade."

We'd had this discussion before. Crimes committed within the park boundaries were clearly our jurisdiction, but rarely did the investigation stay with us. "I've got a few interviews set up. Let's get through those and see where it leads." We both knew if it looked like a slam dunk and would get him on the news, he would let me pursue it.

"Good publicity for the park never hurts."

"Anything else?"

"Short leash, Hunter. I know Robinson can be difficult, but they've just lost one of their own."

I nodded and rose to leave, surprised when I made it out the door without comment. A glance down the hallway told me that Susan was in her office. As badly as I wanted to get out of the building, I turned in the other direction and headed to my corner of the park-service world, where I sat in my office staring at the four walls for a few minutes, until I determined it would be better to face my nemesis immediately than to sit and wait for the confrontation.

"Kurt," she called.

Of all Susan's attributes, her sweet Southern voice was the most misleading. Her outward appearance told you exactly what to expect, but the sound of her voice belied the duplicity behind it. I stepped to the door, cautious not to cross the threshold and enter her lair.

"I know some of the people you might want to talk to. I'd be happy to help."

"Maybe Robinson." The words were out of my mouth before I thought of the implications. I was still worried that her smile might crack her makeup.

"Happy to help."

I repeated my request for Hayward's personnel file and the list of people with access to the schedule and left it at that before I could do any more damage. Heading downstairs, I waved to Mariposa on the way out. Standing outside with no immediate plans, the fatigue of being up all night and the intensity of our early morning paddle started to set in. I preferred to run my cases into the ground, tracking every lead until it was solved. The thrill of the hunt often got me through the sleepless nights, but now, with no immediate direction aside from the interview with Hayward's partner later this afternoon, I craved sleep.

I walked back to my truck, grabbed my bag, and checked the crime scene again on my way to the dock. No one was there, and I wondered how long Martinez would allow the yellow tape to remain in place. It stood out to a passerby as a testament to something bad happening at the park; something he couldn't tolerate. When I talked to Justine later, I would ensure she was finished before allowing Martinez to eradicate the blood stains from the pavement.

Stepping onto the dock, I noticed the FWC boat I'd searched last night was still in place; odd, as Hayward's partner had made a point to say that Robinson had made him work today. The other boat was gone, though, so I assumed he had been assigned a new partner. Looking up at the sky, I saw several thunderheads building offshore. They weren't forecast to hit land, but they rarely obeyed orders and, with the opportunity to inspect the boat again, I took it, knowing a storm would erase whatever evidence it held.

Climbing aboard, I started at the bow, carefully checking every compartment as I worked my way to the console. Leaning over, I opened the hatch and peered inside. It appeared undisturbed from last night. Taking my time, I removed each item and placed it on the deck. I found nothing unusual: fenders, line, safety gear, and several of the gauges used to measure lobster and stone crab. Placing it all back, I went to the wheel and checked the electronics box and small glove compartment. Again, there was nothing of interest.

I had worked my way back to the transom and opened the hatch there, finding an assortment of typical boating gear. Turning back to the console, two metal measuring gauges caught my eye. They appeared identical to the plastic ones in the console and, knowing that both kinds were readily available, thought nothing of it. Stepping off the boat, I was no closer to the killer than before.

Moving across the dock to my boat, I climbed aboard, started the engine and released the lines. Idling out of the small inlet leading to the larger channel, the first thing I saw was the FWC boat in its usual spot by the boat ramp, with Hayward's partner, Jim Scott aboard. Being Monday, business looked to be slow, and I called out to Scott, asking if he would talk to me now.

Looking around, as if Pete Robinson might be wired into Martinez's camera network, he agreed. A minute later, I had my fenders out and coasted up alongside the FWC boat. He tossed me a line, which I tied off to the midships cleat, and shut off the engine. Each sitting in our own vessel, we suffered an uncomfortable moment's silence before he finally invited me over. Climbing over the gunwales, I sat on the starboard side.

"Sorry about all this."

"No problem. I'd like to see justice served on whoever did this. Hayward was my friend as well as partner."

"Any enemies?"

"We're FWC, naturally a lot of folks resent us, but I don't think enough to kill for it."

"I'm thinking whoever did this knew he would be in the parking lot at exactly that day and time." I floated my schedule scenario.

"Likely, but there's a lot of people who know when our shifts change. Poachers, for sure."

I hadn't considered that angle. Knowing when the officers went on and off duty would make bringing in illicit fish a lot safer. "Anyone in particular?"

"You work out here. There's a handful of the usual suspects, but they mainly stay down south."

He was right. The southern area of the park near the Card Sound Bridge was a hot spot for smugglers. I assumed it could be the same for poachers. Mostly uninhabited, and with miles of small creeks and canals, this close to Miami it was like a magnet for nefarious behavior.

I'd run out of questions, but just as I was about to hop back across to my boat I saw Chico, one of the local guides. His flats boat with its distinctive poling platform dropped down from plane and started into the channel at an idle. I was at the helm of my boat when he passed. Instead of his usual greeting, he put his head down and looked the other way. I thought about asking Scott if he knew Chico, but decided I might get more information from Chico himself.

5

STEVEN BECKER
A KURT HUNTER MYSTERY
BACKWATER FLATS

Pushing off of Scott's boat, I idled across the way to the fuel dock and tied off at the end closest to the ramp. I waved off Will, since I had topped off the tank yesterday, and called over that I would just be a few minutes. With his boat tied up on the finger pier adjacent to the ramp, Chico was backing down his trailer. I stood to the side and watched.

Without the pressure from the weekend crowds, almost anyone can take their time to launch or retrieve a boat. But watching the ease with which Chico stopped the truck with its rear wheels just touching the water, walked over to his boat, ran it onto the trailer, and hooked it up, I thought the Coast Guard Auxiliary might consider offering a class or at least a YouTube video for it to help the masses I had watched floundering around yesterday. I waited until Chico had pulled his truck to an area off to the side, where a hose was supplied to rinse off the saltwater.

He saw me and waved as I approached. Standing in the cockpit, he sprayed the deck from bow to stern, then washed the engine before handing me the hose and, using the trailer's frame for a step, swung over the gunwale, landing easily on the pavement. I knew he wasn't finished and handed the hose back to allow him to flush the engine, and rinse the hull and trailer.

When he was finished, he reached into his cooler and motioned me to a bench overlooking the channel. Unfortunately, it was in plain sight of the FWC agent.

Cracking the beer he took a sip. "I'd offer you one, but your boss is probably watching."

Martinez's reputation preceded him. "No worries. You hear about the agent that got killed yesterday?"

"Too bad. Not going to say he was one of the nice guys, because they're all a bunch of pricks."

Chico was someone I could count on to be honest. I already knew most of the guides resented the FWC officers, though I wasn't sure why. In most cases, once the FWC knew the guides were legit, the professionals were left alone. By checking for unlicensed charters and recreational anglers' catches, the officers were actually preserving the resource by which the guides made their living. My position was ambivalent. I wasn't going to let illegal activity occur, but neither would I allow the FWC to run off the guides; in other words, simply protect and provide access. From my patrols I knew many of the guides' secret spots and did my best to protect them from both the FWC and the public. Although I was on the water almost every day, I had hoped the guides would be extensions of my eyes and ears out there, but their own paranoia, as well as the reputations of my fellow officers and the ones who had preceded me, had soured the guides to anyone in uniform. Chico was an exception.

When I first arrived on these waters, I was fresh from the Plumas National Forest in Northern California. I had fished the trout in the streams there—most rarely exceeding twelve inches, and many closer to six, what many down here would call bait. Several of the guides had taken my questions about Keys fishing as some kind of encroachment. Chico had always helped me out, and was in a large part responsible for whatever success I'd had here, especially in tossing flies to the resident bonefish and permit two of the prized catch-and-release fish in the park.

He drank again. "Is this, like a formal interview?"

"Nah, I just saw you pull in and thought you might have some ideas."

"We keep our distance. They know I'm licensed and everything I do is catch and release, so they give me plenty of space."

Bonefish, permit, and tarpon were poor table fair, but elusive and excellent fighters. "Any talk on the water about Hayward?"

"Robinson instituted a quota system a while back. That's when they stopped patrolling and started camping out here." He looked across the way at the officer. "If I was looking for information, I might stick around here and talk to the folks they pull over. Heard there's a lot of BS going on."

That was an interesting phrase, but I decided not to push him. "Fishing been good?"

"Water's still hot, won't be until that first front comes through to cool it down. But it'll come, always does." He looked out at the water and drained his beer, ending our discussion.

"Appreciate the insight. Let me know when the bite's on."

"Will do." He crunched the can and tossed it into a recycling bin on the way to his truck.

I watched him walk across the lot, checking that there was no sign of inebriation. Fortunately, Bayfront Park was operated by the county and I had no jurisdiction here, but I would do him the favor of stopping him if I thought he'd had too many. There was something about boaters and beer that I didn't understand. Never being able to drink in the sun and heat without feeling sick, I wondered how most guys did it. From the way Chico walked, I decided he was sober, and waved as he pulled around toward the exit.

Walking across the parking lot to the fuel dock, I thought

about his advice to talk to some of the boaters, but on a Monday morning, the lot was near-empty. I recognized several of the trucks and trailers as belonging to commercial guides and fishermen, most who wouldn't talk to me anyway. Even if I was able to corral someone, with Officer Scott sitting across the way, it would cause immediate friction between the Park Service and FWC, something that would likely hinder the investigation.

Figuring the best thing I could do was get some sleep, I stepped aboard my center console, released the lines, and started across the bay. Reaching the dock in twenty minutes, Adams Key was quiet. I noticed Ray's boat was gone, and even Zero failed to make an appearance as I pulled up to the dock. The only sound was a boat in the distance. From the frequency of the engines, it was coming fast and hard, a dangerous move through the windy pass.

The sound got louder, then quieted as the boat entered the mangrove-lined channel. I expected the quiet was temporary, as the brush tended to muffle sound. Too soon, the engine noise regained its volume, and I turned just in time to see the quad-powered center console fly out of the channel. I'd been just about to dock, and was still aboard my boat; now I had to decide how to deal with the inevitable wake. Rather than having the boat tossed against the concrete pilings and dock, I pushed down the throttle and spun the wheel away. It was just in time, as the first wave from the wake lifted the boat.

Giving tickets for speed limit and wake zone violations wasn't usually my thing, but as the second wave lifted the boat, anger rose in my gut. I didn't so much care if the offending boat grounded; it was concern for the safety of other boaters and property that caused me to slam down the throttle and follow. Any oddsmaker would have given me a zero chance of catching the much-faster boat and, without a light bar above the T-top, the only thing that would indicate to the speeding boat that I was the law was the forest-green fabric of the canopy, a signature of the park service, and the hailer, a new addition.

Steering with one hand, I yanked the microphone from its holder and turned the radio to "hail." Keying the button, I called out for the boat to stop. There was no reaction and, thinking they hadn't heard me over the engine noise, I switched the dial to "siren." Keying the microphone again, I heard a single blip. I held it down, and allowed the siren to blast. There was no question that it was loud enough, and a few seconds later, I saw a head turn, and finally the boat slowed.

Pirates of the Caribbean might have been a Disney movie, but there was a very real risk when approaching this new generation of go-fast boats. It was a good sign that they had stopped, and I hoped this was just an overzealous boater at the helm rather than a smuggler. Running up to the larger boat with my starboard side to his port, I tossed the fenders, and called over to the two men aboard to grab the lines. The feeling of dread eased as I saw their faces, and expected my hunch was correct.

"Kurt Hunter, National Park Service," I called over the gap.

"What can we do for you?" the man asked.

There was no discernible accent and he appeared amiable. "You realize how fast you were going through the creek?"

"Just checking the boat out. Sorry about that."

I gave him a stern warning, but was not in the mood to write a ticket. Martinez might have appreciated the revenue but, unlike the FWC, he had yet to institute a quota on citations. That gave me an idea.

"Y'all ever get stopped by the fish and game guys at Bayfront Park?"

They looked at each other and shook their heads. "We're kinda new to this."

I wasn't about to rant about quad-powered outboards and novice boaters, but they might be the perfect pair to get me some information. "I'll let you go with a warning, but I need something in return." From their expressions I could tell I had their attention. I reached into my pocket and pulled out two cards. Reaching across the gunwales. I handed one to each of them. "See what you can find out about those FWC guys and give me a call."

"What, like get pulled over or something? We don't even have any fishing rods."

"No, nothing like that. Just hang out at the ramp and wait until they pull someone over. Then see if some of the boaters will talk to you."

"Like a survey?"

Now they were getting it. "Exactly. Give me a call later, and watch your speed around here."

I had no doubt they would cooperate. It was either that, or have one eye scanning the water looking for me the next time they came out. Aside from Bayfront Park, there were only a few other places to launch in this part of the county. The chances of them running into me at some point were pretty good.

Removing the lines, I tossed them across and idled away. Once clear, I pulled in the fenders, and headed back to Adams Key, hoping to get some rest.

Ray's boat was at the dock when I returned. He and Becky were unloading groceries while Jamie played with Zero. They had a strange look about them. "Hey," I called out as Ray came over to help with the lines.

"Heard about the FWC guy getting killed," he said.

Though he preferred to stay away from headquarters, and the mainland in general, Ray was as wired into the coconut telegraph as anyone. "Yeah, got any ideas?"

"That whole office, from Robinson down, is crooked."

"Yeah, I don't like the way they set up shop across from the ramp and just pull random people over."

"Cross between a speed trap and a DUI checkpoint, if you ask me," Ray said, shaking his head.

Forgetting the fancy name Justine had called them, I remembered the soft pieces of lobster I'd seen in the cooler. "You know what they do with the stuff they confiscate?"

"That's a good question. Seen them taking shorts off people, but never did think what they do with them."

"Wouldn't think it amounts to enough to kill someone over."

"People been done in for less, but I hear you there. Unless they got a big score, but the guys setting up them casitas'd be smarter than to run in there. Plenty of other spots to offload if you weren't wanting attention."

Ray had been my educator when I first moved here: from teaching me about the passes and creeks the smugglers preferred to the illegal casitas—man-made habitats used by poachers to draw in lobster—as well as where and how to fish these waters. Patrolling his hot spots had netted me more than a few arrests.

With Becky now well into her third trimester, I helped Ray with the groceries, then headed across the clearing to my house. Just as I reached the door, my phone rang. Glancing down, I didn't recognize the number, but it was a local area code and I thought about the two yahoos I had just given my card to.

"Hunter," I answered.

"We done what you asked, but we didn't need to talk to no one. Son of a bitch pulled us over on the way in, and he was a damned site meaner than you."

BACKWATER FLATS

"Slow down, and tell me what happened." They were both talking at the same time and I assumed they were on speaker. One account would have been preferable, but I didn't want to stop them.

"We was coming in the channel, nice and slow like you told us, and this dude flashes his light bar and calls out over his loudspeaker that we should idle toward his boat. We got over there and he started doing a safety inspection."

The voice changed. "Can they do that? I thought it was fish and game. You seen us. There weren't a rod on board."

"Some folks'll fish with traps." I wanted to end that rant and find out what had happened. "A big center console like yours with four outboards and outriggers—it's quite the fishing machine; I can see why he would check you out."

The compliment slowed them down. "So, what happened?" I asked.

"Shoot, we got all that stuff. Ain't nothing he could have done. Son of a bitch ran our drivers' licenses when he couldn't find anything else. "

"Did he check your coolers and fish boxes?"

"Sure enough, but they're empty. Didn't even bring no beer this trip."

"I really appreciate your help. If you think of anything else, please let me know."

They hung up, leaving me to wonder if it was standard procedure for the FWC randomly to check safety gear and registrations. Their *modus operandi* seemed to border on harassment. There was always the possibility that the officer could have been influenced by the two rednecks running a mid-six-figure boat. Profiling worked both ways. I thought about who I could call and verify if this was normal operations or not. Robinson was out of the question, and there was no one else within the agency who would trust me enough to give a straight answer.

Susan's offer came to mind. I found her number in my contacts and pressed connect. The minute she answered I realized the decision to involve her was an indictment of how tired I was.

"Funny you calling," she said.

The background noise told me she was in a bar, which gave me an excuse to end the call and figure out how to deal with my mistake.

"Maybe tomorrow morning we can go over some things," I said, deciding it would be better to talk to her sober.

"That'd be good. I know I've gone off the reservation before, but I think I can help you with this case."

I heard someone in the background, and was damned near sure it was Pete Robinson. Neither her location or company were a surprise, and I wondered if there might be something to be gained from my following Robinson. I had called Susan on her work phone, and as with mine, Martinez had permanently enabled location tracking. In this case, it would work to my advantage.

"Nine tomorrow morning. Your office," I said, and disconnected before she could reply. Standing in front of the open refrigerator, I realized how hungry I was, and, eyeing the steaks, pulled them out. It was early for dinner, but I'd been up all night. I texted Justine that I was going to eat and go to bed. She acknowledged with a smiley face emoji and a comment about wearing me out this morning. I called my work day complete, grabbed a beer, and carried the steaks outside to the grill.

Sitting on the porch, sipping the cold beer and smelling the fat as it dripped and drizzled onto the grill, I tried to think about anything but the case. I'd been here before, where I was so focused on results that I couldn't see the forest through the trees. In my previous life, the same kind of thinking had cost me my family.

My best work was done cruising the flats and checking out the barrier islands. Yeah, I tossed a few lines, which wasn't exactly procedure, but when I fished I became one with nature, and often saw things I would ordinarily miss; both crimes and clues. I'd started doing this back in the Plumas National Forest in California. In the same methodical way that I now patrolled the waters of Biscayne National Park, I had used an ATV in Plumas. In my work, I'd discovered wilderness, whether water or land, held magnets; water in the forest, and land on the water.

A lifetime ago, while walking the streams of the Plumas wilderness with my fly rod in hand, I had found a strange eddy swirling behind a rock. Checking it out, I realized that there was something pulling water from the stream, and on further investigation found a concealed irrigation line running uphill. I followed it to what—at the time—was the biggest pot-grow ever found on federal land. In hindsight, I should have reported it to the DEA and spared my family the wrath of the cartel whom it belonged to.

Hoping I had learned my lesson, I tried to relax and think

about the fishing and diving trip that Allie, Justine, and I were planning for next weekend. Finally, I was able to fall asleep—for a few hours.

I knew enough to set my phone to "do not disturb," but the two numbers it didn't block were Justine's and Allie's. I expected it was Allie, checking in with her typical "SUP?", but it was Justine.

"Hey."

"Oh crap, did I wake you?"

"Nah."

"Typical male answer. Sorry." She paused. "Anyway. I got the forensics processed and the report back from Sid. I don't think it was a knife that killed him. Sid thinks it's a blunt object, about four inches long, with barbs or points."

I was wide awake now. Knives were hard to place. If the weapon was found, it would need to have forensic evidence intact. It wasn't like a gun, where each barrel had a specific signature that could be matched to the bullet. The weapon Justine described sounded unique, hopefully something that the killer wouldn't discard. I was excited, but it was still like finding a needle in a haystack.

"Any ideas?"

"Fishing, boating, diving ... Think about it."

At least a half-dozen things popped into my mind—all hard to tie to a killer. "Okay." I hoped I wasn't sounding too pessimistic.

"O. M. G. Do I have to come down there and hold your hand?"

I had no idea what she was so worked up about, but the last comment might lead to someplace I'd rather be. "Please. Maybe I'm tired, but I'm not getting it."

"Okay, kemosabe. I'm off tomorrow. Get some sleep, I'll see ya in a few hours."

That made my night, and I easily fell back to sleep thinking about her.

THE ENTIRE DEFENSIVE PERIMETER FAILED. Zero and I both slept through Justine's arrival. The equilibrium of the mattress shifting woke me from a deep sleep. Looking up, I saw Justine and reached for her, but she pulled away.

"Not so fast, lover boy," she said, pecking me on the cheek and rising to evade my grasp. "We've got work to do."

I rubbed my eyes, but gave no response.

"Like finding a murder weapon—hello."

"I thought it was your day off?"

She reached into her bag and tossed a stack of eight-by-ten pictures on the bed. Each was a shot of the wound, taken from different angles, with a tape measure set beside the gash. Even I could see the rough edges and bruising around the penetration area. It certainly wasn't a sharp knife that had done this.

"Where do we start?"

"Breakfast. I'm starved." Seeing no reaction from me, she knew if there was no sex involved, the next-best bet to get me going was food. "I'll make a steak omelette."

I put both feet on the ground and rose. "I ate one last night."

"No worries. I'll whip something up. Now get moving."

Still groggy, it took two cups of coffee to jump-start me. Justine dished the omelette onto two plates, and set them on the counter. Now that I was awake, I was eager to hear what she had in mind. Before her call last night, I had no idea what my next step would be; probably tracking down the victim's friends, family, and coworkers. I rarely got results from this time-consuming effort. Maybe some detectives could read people better than me, but from my experience, evidence solved crimes.

"Where do you want to start?" I pushed my empty plate away, then thought better of it and walked around to the kitchen-side of the counter, where I cleaned the omelet pan and our plates.

"How about that mess you call a tackle box?"

Even though her ultimate goal was not to organize my tackle, you had to love a wife who would sort through your fishing gear. We left the house and went down to the small shed built under the deck. Pulling the two boxes and a bin out, I carried them to one of the picnic tables in the day-use area.

I knew what she was after, but in order to accomplish it, everything had to be dumped out. Starting with the tangle of hooks, weights, lures, and tools, I started to separate and organize the smaller items while she studied the bigger tools. Taking a pair of pliers in hand, she simulated stabbing someone. Not satisfied with the result, she tried the same procedure with a dehooker. The bait knife was set to the side, as it was already ruled out, as were the small scissors I used to cut braided line.

Fifteen minutes later, although I was feeling better about myself for cleaning up the mess, we were no closer to an answer. But I knew solutions often came from elimination. Picking up the boxes, I carried them back to the shed and pulled out our dive gear. The larger pieces—buoyancy compensator, regulator, mask, and fins—were set to the side. The closest thing to a possible murder weapon was the snorkel, but the bendable plastic didn't have a chance of penetrating skin. Moving to the smaller items we often carried, I eliminated the knives first. All that was left were compasses on retractable lanyards and a few dive slates used to communicate underwater. I had a small waterproof camera upstairs, but again, it wasn't close to being a weapon.

"Not getting anywhere," I commented while I repacked the gear.

"Put that all away and meet me on the boat." Justine got up and walked toward the dock.

After hanging the bags in the shed, I followed. Tied behind my park service boat was a similar center console that Justine and I recently had bought, and usually docked in a rented slip by her condo on the Miami River. Only a dozen miles as the crow flies, when the weather cooperated as it had today, it was often easier and faster to commute by boat. When the seas were rough, the better option was the longer route, although that meant dealing with Miami traffic and then a shorter ride across the bay.

Ray's boat was gone, possibly explaining why Zero hadn't joined us. Glancing back at their house, it didn't look like anyone was home. It was a little unusual for the family to be gone this early, especially since I had helped with their weekly grocery run yesterday. Setting those thoughts aside, I stepped down into my park service boat.

Justine was riffling through the built-in compartments. I started with the interior of the console. After pulling out the safety gear, there wasn't much else left except for two mesh nets and tickle sticks. The two-foot-long, narrow aluminum sticks were used to tickle the lobster from their cover and the net was used to trap them. Hanging from the end of the sticks were the standard measuring gauges divers and snorkelers were required to carry. By law, lobster needed to be measured while in the water. Shorts and females, identified by the egg sack on the underside of their tails, were released. Another mesh bag that we used to carry the lobster to the surface was with the gear.

Justine picked up one of the tickle sticks and jabbed with it. It might pierce someone's skin, but there was no way it was the murder weapon. Before she set them down, though, I focused on the attached gauges.

"What about the gauges?" I asked.

"They're plastic. I don't see one doing that kind of damage."

She was right. But then I remembered seeing the metal ones aboard the FWC boat. Those could.

7

STEVEN BECKER
A KURT HUNTER MYSTERY
BACKWATER FLATS

"What if it was made from metal?"

She picked up the gauge and ran her fingers along the edges. An inch wide, the gauge was about five inches long with a three-inch notch for measuring the carapace of the lobster. The outside edges of the gauge were slightly rounded, but the inside notch had sharp edges with ninety-degree corners. Justine grabbed the gauge by the end and started thrusting it in a stabbing motion.

"It would've had to catch the skin on the inside edge. I don't see how it's possible." She handed the gauge back to me.

Justine had thrust with an in-out stabbing motion. "You're striking out like a girl." I knew that comment was a mistake, but she took no offense—for now.

"Holding a knife with the blade facing down, you're more likely to cut yourself than your opponent." I turned the gauge over, and with an underhand motion slashed up.

"That'll do it. Especially with the added cargo he was carrying."

The visual wasn't pretty, but Hayward had been close to fifty pounds overweight. If it had caught on the underside of his paunch, the sharp, inside edge of the gauge could have easily pierced his skin. The ragged wound Hayward had died from might very well have been made by the gauge.

"I think we have it. Thank you."

We both stared at the gauge. "We should send a picture to Sid and see if he agrees," Justine said.

I picked up my phone and snapped a picture, which I messaged Sid. "Now for the big question. Why would you kill someone with a lobster gauge?"

"It was handy?"

That meant the crime might have been more of an emotional response to provocation rather than a premeditated murder. The distinction fell along the lines of preparation: You don't bring a knife to a gun fight, or a lobster gauge to a cold-blooded murder.

As Justine and I sat on the gunwale, wrapped up in our thoughts, my phone dinged. Reaching into my pocket, I fished it out, hoping it was Sid.

"What is this, a work date?" Martinez's voice blasted across the bay. "How cute."

Instinctively, I looked up at the camera mounted just below the security light. The dock was technically a public access point for the day-use area, so in his mind he had a right to snoop. I felt differently. Before I could respond that we were working, he started again.

"And why are you messing around in the internal workings of the FWC?"

"The internal workings? I'm just asking a few questions."

"Tread lightly, my friend. You of all people know about inter-agency squabbles."

I had to assume he was talking about my relationship with

Miami-Dade. With the exception of Grace Herrera, I was pretty much *persona non grata* with the police department. Before I could explain that we had discovered the likely murder weapon, he cut me off.

"Susan will be your liaison with the FWC. Let her do the talking." He disconnected.

I'd already made the mistake of asking for her help. There was no way this investigation's communication was going through Susan McLeash. I remembered "ordering" her to meet me this morning, but wasn't concerned, as she had probably forgotten about it with her next drink.

Justine had a questioning look on her face. "Martinez?"

I nodded.

"Crap."

She was more than familiar with my publicity-seeking boss and his annoying sidekick. At first, she'd thought I was overreacting, but over time she had observed what I had to deal with.

"He wants Susan to be the liaison with the FWC."

"So, use her."

I thought her statement was a reprimand for being obstinate about accepting help, but after thinking about it for a minute, I realized if Susan asked the hard questions, she would take the brunt of their anger. "Like, shoot the messenger."

She winked. "Smarter than you look."

"Martinez already thinks we're taking a day off. We shouldn't disappoint him."

"I'm in for that. What do you want to do?"

"I've got lobster on my mind. Wanna see if we can rustle some up for dinner?"

"Sounds good. Let's grab the gear and hit the reef."

We took two tanks and a hookah rig that Ray had recently fashioned. It allowed a twenty-five-foot hose to be attached to a tank, which floated on the surface. With our other gear, the front deck of the boat was crowded, but we'd done this plenty of times. Grabbing two spinning rods—just in case—we packed a cooler and headed northeast, following along the inside of Elliot Key.

With our discovery of the possible murder weapon, this trip could be justified as work. The only problem was, we would have to leave the bay to hunt, as lobster were protected in the Biscayne Bay/Card Sound Lobster Sanctuary, which encompassed the inside waters of the park. Most of my time was spent inside the boundary islands, leaving the outside to the FWC and ICE. Martinez had trackers aboard the boats and would know where we had gone. When he asked for an explanation, I needed to have one ready.

"Where're we headed?" Justine asked.

She had expected us to go out Caesar Creek. Just outside the pass we would be in the vicinity of some nice coral heads that I knew often held lobster, but on a quiet Monday I wanted to do some exploring and check out one of the less-traveled routes to the ocean.

"I was thinking about heading out the pass between Elliot and Sands Keys. There's some coral heads not too far offshore."

The boat was powered by an older hundred-fifty horsepower outboard. The newer models were much quieter, but this motor was still serviceable and wouldn't be replaced until it failed. Between the wind created by the twenty knots we were traveling, the sound of the water against the hull, and the engine itself, it was hard to talk. Glancing over at Justine, I could see she was enjoying the ride as much as I was. There's something about running wide open over calm seas on a warm sunny day with a beautiful woman beside you that takes away whatever pains a man.

I slowed for the pass and slipped easily between the two

markers outlining the deep-water channel. Once we were clear, Justine climbed up the T-top for a better view of the bottom. At midday from ten feet above the water the definition is striking. Top-to-bottom visibility lasted until we were just past twenty-five feet of water. She pointed out a promising coral grouping ahead. Slowing to follow her directions, I circled the spot and she tossed a buoy with a nylon line and four-pound weight attached to mark the location. In order to get the stern of the boat over the area, I set the engine in neutral and watched the drift as it moved us to the southwest. On the reciprocal heading, I passed over the buoy and traveled about a hundred feet beyond, where we dropped anchor. A quick nudge into reverse set the hook, and Justine paid out the rode as we drifted back toward the buoy. Once we were a few feet from it, she secured the line.

Standing in the bow, I could clearly see the large, round coral heads rising from the bottom. Out west, after the runoff from the snow melt (when the water was a turgid mess) was over, the streams were equally clear, but they were only several feet deep; here, the depth finder showed us in twenty-three feet. Had I not known that, just looking down through the water, I would have expected to be able to reach over the gunwale and touch the bottom.

Justine had been playing around with freediving and donned a pair of extra-long fins that would propel her to the bottom with minimal effort and oxygen use. She sprayed our homemade defogger, a mixture of baby shampoo and water, into her mask, rinsed it out, and placed it over her head. While I was attaching the first stage of the hookah rig to the tank, she slid into the water.

I stopped to watch her, knowing how dangerous freediving actually is. Advanced divers can hold their breath for several minutes. Justine and I had challenged one another, with my dropping out at just over a minute; she lasted close to two and I think she could have gone longer. Despite her prowess, she told me her contractions generally start toward the middle of the second minute. Though not dangerous in themselves, they are a warning sign and if ignored for too long there is a real danger of shallow-water blackout.

We exchanged glances before she tilted her head down and, with one leg straight and the other bent, she slipped under the surface. Once submerged, with two graceful kicks, she leveled off, hovering just over the bottom. With one eye on her, I tossed the tank, which was surrounded by a foam sleeve, into the water. After feeding out the air hose, I donned my own gear and, with a tickle stick, net, and bag in hand, dropped over the side.

We passed each other, me going down and her coming up. After exchanging okay signs we continued on our paths. I'd learned from prior excursions to add extra weight to my belt if we were hunting lobsters. It was important to be able to rest on the bottom while you enticed the crustaceans from their holes. Gently, so as not to disturb the sand, I dropped to the bottom and, using my hands, walked my way to the first coral head. The area we were on was comprised of singular, hump-shaped pieces of coral, set several feet apart with patches of sand in between. Most were hollow—perfect hiding spots for fish, moray eels, and lobster.

Several lion fish were in the first head I checked. On my next trip to the surface I would grab the small Hawaiian sling, a simple sling-shot type device suitable for spearing the slow-swimming fish. As easy as they are to harvest, the invasive species is out of control on many of the South Florida reefs. With their razor-sharp, venomous spines, they have no natural predators. They reproduce with wild abandon and have decimated several native fish populations, including grouper. Tournaments and challenges were springing up all over to collect them, and over the last year I thought I had noticed a small decline in their population.

Justine was back and together we scoped out the next coral structure. This one was larger and, from several feet away, I could see a half-dozen antenna probing the waters outside of the shelter. We looked at each other and I handed her the stick and net. Easing herself up to the opening, I watched as she extended the tickle stick into the hole. From my vantage point I couldn't see what she was doing, but knew from the flick of her wrist and the position she held the net that she had the stick behind one of the bugs. Prodded from behind, it slowly walked out of the hole. I could just about see the head when Justine positioned the net and, with a swoop of the stick, forced the lobster from its cover and into the net.

The battle is not over until the bug's in the bag and Justine wasted no time dropping the stick and grabbing the carapace through the outside of the net. Once she had a firm hold, she started to shake it back and forth, disorienting it. The movement dislodged the small grain of sand in its brain that told the crawfish if it was right-side up or upside down. It stopped fighting and started to relax—at least for a second. I moved into position and opened the mesh bag. With one hand on either side of the net, Justine worked the critter free of the net's webbing. With a death grip on the lobster she positioned it tail first, stuck her hand inside my bag and released it. Lobster walk forward, but swim backwards, and I soon felt a thud as it hit the back of the bag. Before the bug could recover I closed the bag.

Without a regulator, I could see the smile on Justine's face when she looked at me. Taking a deep breath from my regulator, I removed it from my mouth and handed it to her. Rather than surface for air, she gratefully accepted it. Once she had recovered, we changed roles and I netted the next lobster. Warned by the rasping sound its netted compatriots made by scraping their antenna across their carapace, the third lobster bolted from the cover of the coral head and disappeared.

We smiled at each other and moved to the next structure. Not having the burden of pulling the hose and tank behind her, Justine reached the opening first, but quickly backpedaled. I could see the shock in her eyes as she moved away.

8

Justine quickly recovered and made a swooping motion with her hand, the sign for an eel. Morays like the same cover as lobster and are generally benign, except for the larger ones. As this one moved out of the hole, hopeful for a meal, we could see six feet of eel already and still no tail. We both swam to the side, knowing the eels preferred to hunt near their homes. With a dose more caution this time, Justine approached the next hole.

We proceeded like this for maybe forty minutes—until I felt a restriction in the air line. Surfacing, I could feel the weight of the seven or eight lobsters we'd caught in the bag. We ended up about a hundred yards from the boat, and I was glad there was little current as I kicked back. Hauling the bag out of the water, I tossed it on the deck and climbed aboard. Reaching behind me, I took Justine's fins from her and offered a hand, which she declined.

"Nice job. I counted eight, what do we have?"

After quickly stowing the gear, I dumped the bag out on the deck. "Eight it is."

"You know what? We never measured them."

Whether this had any relevance to the case, I didn't know,

but it did make me think. "I don't think we've ever measured underwater. You kind of get a sense if they're too small and let those go. As hard as it is to get the buggers into the bag, holding them to measure would risk losing them."

"The point is, we didn't."

Taking the gauge, I slipped it over the hard head of each lobster. Hooking the leading edge onto the hard spot between the eyes, I placed the other end on the base of the body. Only one was close, while the others were clearly large enough. "Guess we got lucky." I placed the lobsters in the live well and flipped the switch to power it up.

"Want to go for a limit?" In these waters the daily allotment was six per diver per day.

"Nah. That was awesome, though."

I hoped we might be in agreement on the day's next activity and finished putting away the gear. We hung out on the water a while longer, drinking from our water bottles and enjoying the sun.

"I wouldn't have a second thought about tossing one back if it was short." Even though we hadn't measured them in the water, they were still alive when we did.

"Even if it was the only one you caught?" Hitting the limit was not the norm for these waters.

She was right about that. Many days we were lucky to do two dives and bring back one or two lobster. "I think so."

Justine's mind had returned to work mode.

"There were quite a few pleopods in that bag you collected from the boat's cooler. I'm assuming that was just a small percentage that probably fell off on their own."

I thought about what we had just discovered. Penalties for taking shorts were big. First offenders were fined between one- and five-hundred dollars with an added option for up to sixty days in jail. For subsequent offenses the fines tripled and incarceration was likely. Hardly worth it for something you could buy for twenty bucks at a seafood shop.

Justine's comment had me thinking about biology and I pulled one of the lobsters from the live well. The first thing I noticed was each of the ten small appendages, called swimmerets, were still intact. "How many would you guess would fall off naturally?"

"Suppose it would depend on how they were handled. We can put some on ice when we get back and see how hard they are to remove."

I wished I had taken a count, but I did have a picture of the cooler of the FWC boat on my phone. Anxious to find the answer, I started the engine and went forward to pull the anchor. Justine stepped behind the wheel and, following my hand signals, moved us over the anchor as I took in the slack. Once we were directly above it, she cut the power and I pulled it aboard. We were all smiles as we headed back to Adams Key.

In the name of science we left two lobsters aside and cleaned the rest. The remaining pair were placed on ice in the cooler of my center console in an attempt to recreate the conditions I had observed aboard the FWC boat. I put three in the refrigerator for dinner and placed the other three in a Ziploc bag with a small amount of the water from the live well, which went into the freezer. I had learned since coming to Florida that the bad reputation of frozen fish was a misnomer. Properly frozen fish are excellent, but that means freezing them immediately after cleaning and ensconcing them in a seawater or saltwater slurry to ward off freezer burn.

With several hours to spend before our experiment needed to be checked on, I grabbed Justine and led her back to the bedroom.

I COULD TELL by the shadow across the window that I had fallen asleep, and lazily dragged my arm across the other side of the bed, only to find it empty. Getting up, I dressed and, not seeing Justine in the house, went outside. The deck was deserted and only the three center consoles were at the dock. I silently thanked Ray for his quiet return and headed downstairs. As I expected, one of the paddleboards was missing.

Scanning the water, I saw no sign of Justine, but that was to be expected. She could move the board at a steady five miles per hour and was likely back in the lagoon. I glanced over at the cooler holding the lobster on my boat, but decided to wait until Justine was with me to unveil the result of our experiment. Thinking I'd get a start on dinner, I had just turned toward the house when I heard the screen door of Ray's house open and Zero's toenails scratch the weathered wood as he plodded down the steps.

He reached the bottom, eyed me, and, scanning the dock and grounds, sniffed the air.

"Just me, buddy," I called to him.

Slowly he waddled over, not showing nearly the excitement he did when Justine or Allie was here. Thinking about Allie, I rose and sent her a quick "what's up" text. I slid the phone back in my pocket and turned toward the dock as I heard footsteps behind me.

"Y'all get out today?" Ray asked.

I had to think for a few seconds before I realized that he had seen our personal center console docked and guessed that Justine was here. "Yup, got some lobsters off those coral heads behind Sands Key."

"Good spot. Not too picked over, either."

We stood looking at each other for a long second. Ray wasn't hard to talk to, but neither of us had that innate ability to keep a conversation going. A ding came from my pocket before I could think of something to say, and I pulled my cell out. Glancing at the screen, I saw Allie had responded.

"Lucky you have a little one," I said, reading the message. "Allie wants to bring a friend out this weekend."

"Awkward, huh? Boy or girl?"

"Good question." I texted her, asking who.

"Them little ones ain't no picnic, either."

I finished my text and looked up at him.

"Preschool and such. Becky thinks Jamie needs to be socialized."

"That's a bad thing?" I asked.

"It is if we have to move across the bay."

I could see the distress on his face. This was a comfortable home for him, but getting a kid to school from the island would be a chore, especially when the weather didn't cooperate. Before I could think of the implications of his statement, I saw a figure skimming across the water. Justine was digging hard to overcome the tidal current running through Caesar Creek and quickly coasted up to the dock.

Zero immediately perked up and ran down to greet her.

"How long you got?" I asked Ray, realizing I had said it like it was a prison sentence.

"She's thinking after Christmas."

We both looked down and shook our heads, knowing what it meant for both of us. Ray would lose his dream home and I would have a new neighbor. Maybe it was worth a conversation with Justine about moving to a larger place on the water that would be an easier commute for both of us, but I put that thought aside. I liked my island.

"Did you check them?" Justine asked as she stepped onto the dock. Ignoring Zero, she pulled the board from the water and set it on the dock, where she leaned it against the concrete pilings and hosed the saltwater off.

"No, I was waiting for you." She probably guessed that I had just woken up, so I left it unsaid. My phone dinged again. "Allie wants to bring a girlfriend out this weekend."

"Cool, that'll be fun."

I was thankful that it wasn't a boy, but also felt awkward around her girlfriends. "So, I'll tell her okay?"

"Heck, yeah. It'll be a girls' weekend."

Exactly what I didn't want. I texted Allie that it would be fine and met Justine, who had just put the board and paddle away, at the center console. Ray tagged along behind us.

"What y'all got?" he asked.

"A little experiment." I told him about the cooler on the FWC boat.

The three of us gathered around the cooler, not sure what to do. Finally, Justine opened the lid to remove one of the lobsters from the ice. It stuck enough to pull off two of the small swimmerets. The other lobster yielded the same result.

"Okay, so two for each. How many do you think there were on the FWC boat?"

I pulled out my phone, opened the picture I had taken, and zoomed in. Placing it between us, we started counting. It was tedious work and I thought about sending the image to my computer's larger screen, but then remembered something I'd read about how to estimate crowd size. By dividing the picture into ten sections, I quickly counted twelve swimmerets in one section. Multiplying by ten gave me a hundred-twenty. Justine, using her own method, thought there were more.

"Plus the dozen or so I put in the evidence bag, divided by two ... that makes sixty lobster," I said.

"That's a whole lot of stupid people. Any fool knows those FWC clowns sit there every day," Ray said.

That about summed it up. Unless they had made one huge score, which was possible, something was wrong.

"You know what they do with the confiscated catch?" I asked Ray.

"Darned good question. I'd expect, knowing our government, they'd find their way to a dumpster after being counted and recorded. Sure ain't feedin' the homeless."

I thought he was right about that as well, but still couldn't see someone tossing over twelve hundred dollars' worth of lobster in the trash. Allowing that the "speed trap" was happening every weekend, and subtracting a couple days a month for bad weather, equaled six or seven days a month for lobster confiscation. Multiplying that by the eight months that lobster are in season gave me a sum total north of sixty-thousand dollars in lobster meat.

"I think we found a motive."

STEVEN BECKER
A KURT HUNTER MYSTERY
BACKWATER FLATS

"So, you're thinking Hayward was in on some kind of scam?" Martinez asked dismissively.

I'd waited until morning, but I'd had no choice but to report in. We'd done this dance before. If there was going to be no glory, there would be no investigation. Several times Martinez had tried to shut me down by transferring an active case to another jurisdiction. His numbers looked better for it, but this method left me without closure on many of my cases. I had a feeling I was onto something now, and wasn't going to let Martinez get away with it this time.

"You've said that you don't like them operating in the park." I'd hoped to rattle his cage by making this a revenue issue. If the FWC was writing tickets to boaters, the park service wasn't.

He turned away from his monitors, placed his hands on his desk, and leaned forward. It was clearly a move to intimidate me. In a backhanded way, he got what he wanted. In my mind I saw myself leaning forward, placing my hands on the desk across from his, and meeting his gaze, but instead the golf trophies on his shelf caught my attention. I had long suspected they were frauds, maybe purchased at a trophy shop and prominently placed on display. Remembering who I was dealing with, I leaned back and crossed my legs—the opposite reaction to what he expected from me.

Living on an island you get to read a lot. I'd downloaded a copy of Marcus Aurelius's comments on life titled *The Emperor's Handbook*. I recalled one of my favorite passages from the Stoic's guide: *The first rule is to keep an untroubled spirit; the second is to look things in the face and know them for what they are*. The golf trophies were just a reminder of who my boss was.

"This could work out to our advantage."

He backed away slightly. "It's always a good idea to think of the department first."

I had made contact and was rounding first base.

"It would be more revenue for the park."

He was clearly interested. "A lobster reclamation program." I was about to slide into second, but from his expression, I thought the play might beat me. Before he could pass judgment, I blurted out my half-baked plan.

"We take the shorts from the FWC and place them back in the Biscayne/Card Sound Sanctuary. Could be a lot of good publicity."

The ball skidded off the base just out of reach of the shortstop. I was safe at second.

"This could be something Susan would be good at." The pitcher wound up and threw a wild pitch past the catcher. I easily pulled up at third base.

"Keep talking."

"Given Susan's relationship with Robinson and his crew, she'd head up the effort for the park. It would only take a few tanks to hold the shorts we confiscate, and we could put them on display in the welcome center. Might be a big draw."

"Sounds like the cost would be minimal." He steepled his fingers together and leaned back, calculating revenue, less expenses, multiplied by exposure. As he leaned towards his monitors, I thought I had lost him until he picked up the phone and hit a single button.

"Susan. Can you come in here, please," he spoke into the handset.

I almost commented aloud, but kept it to myself. I don't recall him ever using that last word with me. Again, a glance at the fake golf trophies reminded me who I was dealing with, and I breathed deeply, trying to relax.

Susan entered the office and took her usual chair.

"We would like to leverage your relationship with Robinson and the FWC to spearhead a joint project."

He made putting some lobsters in a tank and releasing them a few miles from here sound important.

"Sounds interesting. We'd have to adjust my workload accordingly," Susan said.

Listening to these two public employees who had mastered the system, I almost reached for my pad to take notes. Martinez went on to explain my proposal, doing his best to make it seem like his own. The subject of what the FWC was presently doing with the shorts never came up.

Robinson's reaction to the proposal would be interesting. "I'd like to be there when you present the idea," I said.

Susan turned to look at me, and then at Martinez, who read her expression and backed her up. "That won't be necessary, Hunter. You just keep working the case."

"Any leads?" Susan asked.

I had to tell her about the lobster gauge being a strong possibility for the murder weapon. Pausing, I wondered if I should share my theory that the shorts were being sold, figuring that Martinez would tell her the second I was gone.

The two batters behind me had struck out and the coach signaled a hit and run. I had nothing left to lose, and told her. I'd expected her to laugh it off, protecting her friends, but she was quiet, leading me to believe that she already knew or, at least, suspected something.

"Alright, back to work, everyone," Martinez said, turning back to his monitors.

I took that as a dismissal and rose to leave. Susan was right behind me and stopped me in the hallway.

"You wanted some help? You were going to meet me yesterday." Of course, she remembered.

"It's nothing, really." I started walking away, then changed my mind. She had taken over the lobster reclamation program like it was a promotion. If there was ever a good time to ask her, it would be now.

"Hayward or any of those guys throwing around money they maybe shouldn't have?"

She looked down. "You really shouldn't talk about the deceased like that." That was as much of an answer as I was going to get out of Susan. Reminding her that I would be happy to meet Robinson later, I walked away thinking the discussion would probably happen in a dimly lit bar—and I would be nowhere close. Back in my office, I fired up the ancient computer. My laptop out at Adams was a much faster machine, but the internet connection there was slower. While my desktop booted up, I grabbed a cup of coffee and checked my phone. There was a message from Allie that her mom would have her and her friend at headquarters around five on Friday. Apparently, her car had broken down a few days ago and was in the shop. I responded that I would be there and turned to the computer.

"Follow the money" was an oft-used phrase for good reason. There would be no waterfront homes bought from this scam, but sixty-grand was enough for a fast car or expensive vacation. Hoping Robinson had followed through on my request, I checked my email first. Surprisingly, there was something from an "Anita" at the FWC. It wasn't the entire file, but it did have Hayward's social security number.

The park service computers had access to several databases and credit agencies. Logging into one, I entered Hayward's name and social. The screen went black for a long second, then started to populate. I scanned the results. Reading between the lines of a credit report was far from an art, but did require some work. Entering his address in the tax collector's website, I obtained a value for his property. It, of course, had to be adjusted for reality, forcing a detour to Zillow, where I got some comps from other, similar houses in his neighborhood. After a few minutes of study, nothing jumped out at me. Average credit score, average debt, average mortgage.

Hoping the coast was clear, I closed and locked my door, and passed Martinez and Susan's offices. I'd reached a point where I had a theory, but not much in the way of evidence to confirm it. When I reached this point in a case, I usually hit the water for inspiration. Thinking a run down to the southern end of the bay, inside the boundaries of the lobster sanctuary, might give me some ideas, I said goodbye to Mariposa and left the building. At the dock, I hopped aboard my boat, started the engine and freed the lines. Idling out of the channel, I was surprised the FWC boat wasn't in its usual lurking place. Thinking back, I didn't recall that it had been docked, either.

I decided it was worth the few minutes to backtrack and check. The twin-engine RHIB was there, but not the center console they used for traffic stops. Retracing my path, I scanned the ramp area and small marina beyond it. There was still no sign of it. I couldn't remember a time when I had seen the boat leave the channel, and decided to stop at the fuel dock and ask Will if he had seen them today.

I waited while he filled a sailboat that was moored in the

small marina behind the ramp to question him.

"Headed out around an hour ago," he answered.

"Ever see them leave the channel before?"

"Back before Robinson, things were different—like they did their jobs instead of harassing people."

I didn't need much fuel, but I decided since it was a slow day I could keep him talking. He'd know there was a tip coming as well—probably the only one he got from the park service people. It was hard handing over the government credit card and then tossing in some of my own cash, but I knew his was a low-paying job and he relied on tips to make it worthwhile. Unlike other members of my department and the FWC, I also thought it was important to make friends.

The sailboat moved off and I pulled the boat forward to take its place. I shut down the engine and removed the key and kill switch from the ignition panel. On the chain was the two-pronged key used to open the gas cap. Once I unscrewed it, Will handed me the pump.

"Probably only needs ten gallons," I warned him. Unlike cars, marine fuel pumps don't stop automatically. An overflow port on the side of the boat warns you seconds before the tank fills.

"Got a big day planned?"

"Nah, just toppin' her off." I could tell he was curious now. I usually never stopped unless the seventy-gallon tank was less than half full.

"Any talk going around about Hayward?" I tried to make it sound like I was just making conversation.

"I watch those guys when we're slow. It's kinda like sport, seeing who's gonna get mad and go off on them."

"What do you mean?" I didn't like writing tickets, but most people were on their best behavior after getting pulled over. There was no point in antagonizing the law.

"I guess y'all are a different department. From what I seen and hear, those guys hand out more tickets for safety violations than fishing stuff."

This was the second time I'd heard that observation. "You'd think they would just be checking fishing licenses and catches."

The gurgling of the tank stopped our conversation. A small stream of gas shot out the overflow, signaling me to shut off the pump. I was a second too late, and gas dribbled over the gunwale. Exchanging the pump for a paper towel, I cleaned up the mess, screwed the cap back in and followed Will to the small building where he ran credit cards. Pulling out the park service card, I handed it to him along with a ten-dollar tip.

"Appreciate it, man."

"Do me a favor and keep an eye on them for me."

"Sure thing, man. Never liked that Hayward dude."

Thinking about what I'd learned, I thanked him and walked back to the boat. Stepping aboard, I could smell gas from the spill, but knew it would dissipate as soon as I started running. I stuck the small plastic piece in the kill switch, inserted the key into the ignition, and started the engine. After resetting the fuel level on the engine gauge, I went to release the lines, but Will was already there to help.

"Hey, did you see which direction he headed?" I asked him.

"South, man."

I nodded and pressed the throttle forward. Cutting the wheel to port, and with an assist from the southerly wind, the boat eased away from the dock. It was tempting to speed up and cut the last two markers. There was no traffic, and being high tide, I knew there was plenty of water, but I curtailed myself. Anyone seeing a park service boat take that route might copy me, and if they did so at a low tide would ground. The blame instantly would fall on me.

10

I WAS TEMPTED TO SPEED ACROSS THE BAY IN SEARCH OF THE FWC boat, but decided if I *did* encounter them, it couldn't *appear* like I was out there looking for them. Instead I steered a southeast heading, holding to 3600 rpms, just enough to keep the underpowered boat on plane. Scanning the water, I crossed to the barrier islands, the beginning of the Upper Keys. Below Old Rhodes Key was an area I checked regularly. The mangrove-lined shore and winding creeks separating the Atlantic and Biscayne Bay were perfect places for nefarious activity.

Though I'd been here often, I still relied on my chartplotter to remind me of the ins and outs of the small islands. Starting at the northern end, I worked my way south, checking each creek along the way. I ran into several guides, none of who were friends, but they all waved just to make it look that way, and not garner any attention. I'd been scouting for a good two hours when I started to think the FWC boat had gone somewhere else. Other scenarios, from taking it for maintenance to a routine patrol, crossed my mind, but I dismissed them. Hayward was dead and something suspicious was going on.

I continued my search, crisscrossing between the Atlantic

and the bay, until finally the northern coast of Key Largo appeared ahead. Wherever they had gone, the boat was either not here or I had missed it.

But there was another area that might be worth checking. Across Cutter Bank I could see Long Arsenicker Key. Midnight Pass was behind it and out of sight; a favorite spot for smugglers.

Transversing the narrowest part of the bay took only a few minutes, and I was about to enter Midnight Pass when I thought I saw the bow of a boat. As it emerged I could see the FWC logo stenciled on its bow flare. I'd found my target, but had no plan. That was taken out of my control when the man at the wheel waved at me, then started to idle in my direction. Excuses ran through my mind until I realized it was less suspicious that I was here than he was.

"Hey, Jim," I called, as I positioned our boat gunwale to gunwale. We were not far enough along in our relationship for fenders, and, not knowing the level of his boating skill, I kept a good three feet between us. He did have enough experience to keep his bow into the current, allowing us to drift together.

"Hunter. What brings you out here?" he asked.

My initial reaction was to ask the same of him, but I thought that might be a touch suspicious. Finally, I eased my attitude, hoping his question was just a conversation starter. "Martinez has me patrol a quadrant a day." I took the easy way out. While we talked, I checked out his boat, but everything seemed to be in order.

"We got a call about some cracker shooting snapper."

"Did you find him?"

"Nah, half the calls we get are smokescreens so the perps know where we are."

We both turned when we heard the unmistakable roar of a cigarette boat coming toward us. The bay is mostly known as a pristine wilderness area, but it is also protected water and, being just a few miles from Miami, is a hot-rodders paradise. We both stopped and listened. The decibels increased, telling me the boat was moving around fifty knots and approaching the pass. I dropped into forward and started to inch away from the FWC boat, hoping to create some distance between the two boats when the inevitable wake found us. We were ten feet apart when the go-fast boat came into view. Seconds later, paying us no mind, it was gone, its only legacy a large wake. Grabbing the stainless-steel supports of the T-top, I held on as the first wave lifted the boat. Fortunately, we were far enough apart now that the destructive wave was neutralized.

But Scott was slow to react, and leaving the FWC boat only five feet away and drifting closer. Before the next wave hit, I slammed the throttle forward to avoid a collision. Just before we separated I looked over to make sure Scott didn't have the same idea, and saw water sloshing out of the cooler. The incident ended our encounter, but I was curious. The only reason for a cooler to be filled with water was to keep something alive in it.

I tried to remember if his boat had a live well. Mine did; it was probably standard equipment. Martinez was not the custom-order type of bureaucrat, a decision I supported until he got *too* cheap. The underpowered center console I drove could have used another fifty horsepower to relieve the strain on the engine. The few off-road vehicles we had to patrol the small land areas of the park were light-duty, two-wheel-drive ATVs. With the pancake-flat terrain here you might think that made sense, until you figured in the mud from the tropical climate that made four-wheel drive a necessity.

Scott and I had met inside the lobster sanctuary and, with the water in the cooler, the pieces started to drop into place. It was too soon for Susan to have acted on my plan, but repopulating the confiscated wildlife was what they should have been doing all along.

The wake had pushed both of our boats near the mangroves and, as I had accelerated first, I was first through the pass. Once I hit the open water, I slowed to look back, but Scott was done chatting and whatever else he had been here for. He waved as he passed and cut the wheel in the direction of Bayfront Park.

Not wanting to follow him, I turned for Adams Key. As I turned, I faced a narrow band of dark clouds to the north. Watching the line for a minute, I could see they were pushing southeast. In front of the storms the wind had shifted, making for a bumpy ride back. By the time I reached the dock the waves had started to whitecap and perpendicular lines of spindrift told me the winds had reached twenty knots—enough for me to call it a day.

Using an aft spring line in addition to the bow and stern lines to keep the boat from blowing forward, I checked the fenders and, dodging the first drops of rain, made a run for the house. Zero must have sensed the weather changes as well and barked meekly from the screened porch of Ray and Becky's house. By the time I made it inside it was a full-blown storm.

While I waited for my laptop to boot up, I checked the weather app on my phone. I already knew the storm was here now, but was more concerned with the long-term forecast. A rainy, windy weekend with Allie and her friend would be difficult. Entertainment was limited out here. With only the equivalent of dial-up internet, the demise of video stores, and with the closest Redbox miles away, there were few options. I liked to read, and that was the only thing that got me through some of the stretches of bad weather. Malls, bowling alleys, movie theaters, and restaurants were a long, wet boat ride away.

Fortunately, it looked like this was a fast-moving front. Tomorrow would be windy, but by Thursday the weather would be back to normal—good news on the child-rearing front.

Settling down with a cold beer and my laptop, I started

doing some random Google searches. My first attempt, *what does the FWC do with shorts,* resulted in a list of their uniform requirements. I had better luck the second time by changing out *shorts* to *confiscated fish*. *Saved for evidence* was the primary answer. I guess they froze the product and waited for trial. Mentions of donating fish and lobster to homeless shelters also appeared.

My casual research had told me that neither of these possibilities was happening in this case. The officers had been handing out tickets for safety, registration, and licensing infractions. Warnings were given for the lobsters, which were confiscated. They were being sold and, for some reason, Hayward had been killed because of it.

Just to verify my theory, I checked with several of the local homeless shelters. All six calls were negative, but one remembered a time several years ago when some fish had been donated to them. There was no need to check Robinson's and Hayward's employment records. I was sure that it happened before they were transferred here.

I also needed to verify that Susan hadn't already planted the idea in Scott's head. When there was something she wanted, the woman was a dog with a bone. Instead of calling, I tried to text her, saving me the pain of hearing her voice. In response to my query if she had talked to the FWC, my phone rang. I had no choice and hit *accept*, then placed the device in speaker mode and set it several feet away from me, as if the distance would protect me from her.

"A little pushy, Hunter."

"Just checking." I didn't want to tell her what I had seen. "So, you haven't?"

"It's on the list, but I've got a stack of paperwork to get through first."

The image of her ensconced behind her desk, papers stacked high in front of her, was clear. I had seen this show before.

"What about the employment and contact info? Have you talked to Robinson?"

"Jeez, Hunter. Give a girl a break. I'll get to it."

I heard the line go dead and, avoiding the urge to throw it against the wall, set the phone down. The noisy tattoo of rain on the metal roof got louder, and I looked outside. The sky had darkened and visibility was only about a foot. Turning back to the living room, I suddenly felt like a caged animal. Effectively a prisoner in my own house, I started pacing.

I glanced at the mostly useless TV and over-stuffed bookshelves, my primary source of entertainment. Even though I worked many more hours than Martinez knew about, I still had a thing about calling it a day before "quitting time." Back at my computer, I stared at the screen. I thought about opening a document to outline the case, but that would just be busy work. With so few facts available, I could easily hold them in my head. What I needed was a break in the case. Most investigations had them; you just never knew when they would happen. My usual process, an unrelenting effort to storm through the evidence until the case was solved, often forced the break to come. Stuck at home with the wind whipping around and rain coming down in sheets, making it idiocy to take my twenty-two-foot boat to the mainland, I felt helpless.

Another beer did nothing to curb my anxiety. I texted Justine with a weather update, telling her we would likely be forced to spend the night in separate beds, which furthered my plunge into darkness. I thought about calling or texting Allie, but I didn't want her to get a sense of my mood. A brilliant flash of lightning was followed by a loud crash of thunder, bright enough to illuminate the interior of the house. The storm was directly overhead now, and I thought it might be a good idea to protect the electronics in the house. Even industrial-strength surge protectors are little defense against a direct lightning strike, and our houses, the lone structures for miles, were easy targets. Grabbing my rain jacket, I descended the stairs and made a run for the electric panel, where I flipped off the main breaker.

Standing under the protection of the eaves, I looked out at the water. Squalls this intense could play tricks on your vision, but I swear I saw something move in front of the dock. I knew it could be an illusion, and remained where I was, trying to focus on the dark blur. It stopped by the dock, moved forward, then appeared again, like a cautious boater approaching a dock. My eyes tried to penetrate the nearly opaque curtain of the rain, but failed, and I thought maybe the shadow was moving away—until lightning flashed again, this time horizontal in the sky. The bright light revealed a boat—the same FWC center console I had seen earlier.

11

STEVEN BECKER
A KURT HUNTER MYSTERY
BACKWATER FLATS

Unsure if it was the percussion from the thunder or my own legs shaking, it felt like the dock was moving underneath me. Another flash of lightning illuminated the FWC boat with Scott at the helm. Between the driving rain and pounding thunder, I had to yell across the ten feet of water that separated us to be heard. Docking in this kind of weather in a protected marina would be difficult; out here with no protection and the strong currents running through Caesar Creek, it was sketchy at best. A twin engine would have made the task simpler, as would a structure not built from concrete, but we had neither. The park service had a thing for permanence and so had built the dock—piers, structure, and surface—from concrete. A small rub-rail was installed horizontally, but it only worked if the combination of the boat's lines and the tide coincided. I yelled for Scott to put out whatever fenders he could, then jumped into my boat to grab mine too.

With the wind blowing the boat away from the dock and the current pulling it forward, Scott manipulated the single engine, pushing ahead to close the gap, then spinning the wheel and reversing to bring the stern in. He was doing everything right, but the conditions were against him and he knew that coming in too hot would damage the boat. To make matters worse, the outgoing tide was near its bottom, and it appeared as if his boat was going to slide under the dock.

A solution occurred to me. Not one I favored but, faced with the circumstances, it was the best option. Tossing my fenders over the outboard side of my boat, I waited for him to close the gap, then caught the lines he tossed over. Several minutes later, with four lines tethering the boats together, we ran for the house.

It would have been an awkward encounter under better circumstances, but with the power out and with his boat holding mine prisoner, it was even more so. I knew that more often than not, murders were committed by someone the victim knew well; Hayward's partner fit that bill nicely. I hope I didn't.

"Come on upstairs," I called back to him without stopping to make sure he followed. It wasn't the rain that pushed me forward, but the sky flashed every few seconds, the lightning striking the outer islands. Once inside the screened porch I relaxed and removed my rain gear.

"Thanks, man. Don't know if I could have done that myself. What the hell were you doing out there, anyway?" Scott asked.

I thought if anyone should be asking that question it should be me. "No problem. I just went outside to shut off the main breaker. An ounce of prevention." The sky turned a brilliant blue for a fat second and we both turned to watch the latest strike.

"What were you doing out there?" I asked.

"Saw a waterspout near the park. Figured this was the best choice."

A tornadic waterspout is harmless when cruising over the

water, until something gets in its way; then they are every bit the damaging equivalent of their land-born cousins.

Water dripped onto the tile floor from Scott's saturated clothes and I wondered why he didn't have rain gear. But then I remembered the boat rarely left the channel. Eyeing him up, I figured he was about my size and, potential murderer or not, I offered him a change of clothes. From the linen closet I handed him a towel and went back to the bedroom and found a pair of shorts and shirt that might fit. Handing them over to him, I waited my turn while he used the bathroom.

Once we both dried off and changed, I invited him into the kitchen and opened two beers. We sat at the counter watching the storm, each of us wondering what to say to the other.

"That neighbor of yours still running traps?" he finally asked me.

"You know Ray, he's got saltwater in his blood. Family life is pushing him to the mainland, though." Something in his expression changed and I started to wonder if quizzing me about Ray was the reason he was here.

"What's your interest?"

"Curious is all. Trying to get a feel for what goes on around here."

Robinson was, and Hayward had been, fixtures in the FWC. Scott was newer to the area than I was. "How long've you been stationed here?"

"Just short of six months. Came across from Tampa."

"Like it?" I asked.

He shook his head. "Takes some getting used to. Miami's a whole lot different, and not in a good way. I hear everyone wants out of the Keys, so maybe that'll be my next stop."

I felt his pain. Robinson had to be every bit as difficult to work for as Martinez. I'd also heard that FWC officers hated the Keys. Along with the myriad of canals and public boat ramps, many hotels and marinas had private facilities, making the island chain difficult to patrol.

"So, why make the move?"

He stared out the window and took a long sip of his beer. I could see the conflict on his face. I knew that look.

"Needed to make a change after busting a bluefin-tuna ring. Sons of bitches threatened my family."

It appeared Officer Scott and I had more in common than I had thought. My transfer here had been akin to a witness protection program for park rangers. My family had been threatened as well. Busting the pot-growing ring in California had cost me my home, which the cartel had firebombed, and my marriage. It was only in the last year that I had been reunited with my daughter, and that was more because of Justine and Daniel J. Viscount, my five-figure attorney, than me.

"I hear you. Same thing happened to me."

Tipping my beer at his near-empty bottle, he nodded and I got two more. We exchanged stories over the next twelve ounces until the storm finally moved on.

"Looks like the weather's gone." He finished the last of his beer and set the empty bottle on the counter. "Appreciate the hospitality."

I walked him out to the dock and helped cast off the lines. Staring at the dark line of clouds moving south and at the wake of his boat moving west, I thought about our encounter. The similarities in our stories were striking and I had to admit I felt a bond with the man, totally the opposite vibe from when I first thought I was drinking with a murderer. Now, looking back at Ray's house, I wondered what the FWC's interest in him was.

As far as I knew Ray played by the rules, though I suspected he was close to the edge. He ran his stone crab traps right on the border between the park and public water, in areas no commercial fisherman would dare. When the difference between an expensive ticket or being legal was a random line on a chart, it wasn't worth the risk for most. Those waters were under-fished, and he often doubled and sometimes tripled the averages the commercial guys were bringing in. Commercial licenses were hard to come by, and I didn't think Ray had one. A residential license allowed five traps for each family member, and I'm pretty sure he counted Zero and the unborn baby in his calculation. Spiny lobster traps were not permitted without a license, but he knew the hot spots and scored a limit every time he left the dock. Same thing. Take the family, if they had residential fishing licenses, and whether they dove or not, their half-dozen counted toward the bag limit. On our salaries, raising a family on one income definitely needed some supplementation. I'd always assumed he sold the catch, but it didn't concern me..

I was about to turn back to my house when I heard a screen door open and Zero's nails click-clacking as he plopped down the stairs. Ray followed behind him and I guessed the question before he asked it.

"What's that prick doing out here?"

"Said he saw a waterspout out by headquarters when he was heading in. Decided this was safer."

"Maybe it wiped out that prick Martinez. He have anything to say for himself?"

I had no intention of telling Ray that the FWC was interested in him. "Nah, we just had a few beers and exchanged war stories until the storm passed."

The investigator in me took control and I asked him, "How's the house hunt going?"

"It's tough. Homestead ain't what it was."

Evidence of what the town had looked like twenty years ago still remained. The economy then had been based around agriculture, both consumables and decorative plants, and Homestead Air Force Base. Now, the fields had been replaced by subdivisions and strip malls and the base was a reserve facility. Homestead had lost its independence and become a bedroom community for Miami. Serviced by the ever-widening turnpike, the price of homes had increased exponentially.

"You guys gonna do it?"

"Not seeing I have any choice. Gotta do what's best for the young'uns."

We stood silent, looking at the ground and shaking our heads. Most men knew the feeling of having their wings clipped.

"If you need any help—" I started.

"We're good. Got my traps out most of the season and the fishing's been pretty good in between."

Lobster season ran August through March, with stone crab starting in October and ending in the middle of May. June and July, the mahi-mahi, locally known as dolphin, ran in large schools not too far offshore.

"Guess you need that income now." There was no evidence of his living a larger lifestyle than was apparent, and I suspected he was hoarding the profits from his operations for a down payment on a house. I wondered how to tell him that he was a person of interest to at least one FWC officer. Buying a big house was going to be pretty visible.

"Gotta do what ya gotta do." He turned away and started back to his place.

Things were starting to come closer to home than I preferred, but investigations have a mind of their own. The thought passed through my head that if Ray knew the FWC was after him, he could have killed Hayward. I tried to discard the idea, but it lingered. A good detective allowed investigations to run their course without inflicting personal bias. I knew I had to be careful how I proceeded.

As Ray called to Zero, who had been hovering nearby me, I waited until the screen door slammed behind them before turning the main breaker back on and heading up the stairs to my house.

With the storm gone, the living room didn't feel quite so stifling. I knew another beer would be one too many to let me get anything accomplished, so I settled for water and started mulling over the events of the last few hours. It seemed my friends had turned into suspects, and my suspects into friends.

Living on a small island, there's a magnetic force that has you constantly checking the weather and, after refilling my glass, I took it outside onto the screened porch and looked out at the bay. The water was flat calm, showing no indication of the violence that had just passed. The sun had broken through the clouds and hovered about four fingers over the horizon. For all the turbulence that preceded it, the sunset was sure to be memorable.

Law enforcement has a way of creeping under your skin and occupying your mind, even when off duty. To forget, some use alcohol; others, like Justine, use exercise to clear their minds. Fishing had always been meditative for me and, with an hour of daylight remaining, I grabbed my fly rod and went downstairs in the hope that tossing a few flies would get the gears in my head moving. Still curious about what Scott had been doing earlier, I hopped aboard my center console, started the engine, released the lines, and pushed off the dock.

I reached a comfortable cruising speed and started running a few degrees north of west to avoid West Arsenicker Key, I soon found myself smiling. The wind-whipped waves were gone, but there was still a sizable swell from the storm. Because a single rogue wave or debris in the water can ruin your day, running a boat at speed mimics many of the elements of a flow experience. That minuscule chance of life-threatening danger adds to the rush of flying over the waves. I let my mind go free as I focused on the water ahead of me. Justine had been helping me learn downwind surfing on a paddleboard, and I found the same techniques applied to even out the ride in a motorboat. The important thing wasn't what was behind you, but rather what lay ahead. Avoiding the steep backs of the swells and staying on top of the waves gave a comfortable and efficient ride.

Before I realized it I was between the water access to the Turkey Point power plant, and Pelican Banks, a shallow shoal. With one eye on the chartplotter and the other on the water, I rounded Mangrove Point, and entered Midnight Pass. Dropping power, I allowed the boat to coast to a stop while I assembled the rod and reel. Chico had mentioned the tarpon were running through the channel and I meant to have a go at one. Checking the leader and tippet, I tied on a Clouser minnow and waited to see how the current affected my drift.

The boat moved quickly to the south and straight through the pass. Repositioning at the top of the channel, I cut the engine and moved to the bow, where I stripped about a hundred feet of line onto the deck and started false casting. Presenting the fly close to the mangrove-lined bank as the boat drifted again through the pass, I felt several small tugs, probably from pinfish. Pulling the fly from the last one, I stripped off another two pulls and snatched the line from the water starting the process over again. Once the inertia from several false casts had all the line in the air, I turned and faced the shoreline, pointing the rod tip in the direction of a depression in the mangroves.

The fly landed inches from the roots and disappeared. Stripping in a dozen feet to draw out whatever might be lurking in the mangroves, I braced myself for a hit and wasn't disappointed when a fish inhaled the fly. Instantly the line came tight, the excess line sliding through my fingers. With only seconds before it reached the protection of the mangroves, I clamped my finger on the line and started reeling. Seconds later, a wake appeared, and the distinctive dorsal fin of a tarpon broke the water. Once the slack was on the reel, I was able to properly fight the fish.

The next few seconds were touch and go. I'd have to turn his head in order to pull the tarpon clear of the network of roots beneath the mangroves without breaking him off. With that much strain on the tippet and leader, there was a good chance of losing him, but if he reached cover he would be gone

12

STEVEN BECKER
A KURT HUNTER MYSTERY
BACKWATER FLATS

THE TWELVE-WEIGHT ROD BENT DOUBLE AND I COULD FEEL THE line stretch as I tried to turn him. It was early in the fight to attempt this kind of control on a large fish, but this close to the mangroves I had no choice. His head shook in a violent effort to free the hook. I used the few seconds of the tarpon's indecision and, with my finger on the line to secure it, swung the rod tip to the side. He started to pull, but I reeled in the slack and gave the rod another hard tug again. Suddenly I felt the tension release, and thought I had lost him, but a second later the wake appeared, this time moving away from the mangroves. With that obstacle cleared, I let him take line, giving myself a few seconds to catch my breath and also hopefully to tire the fish.

He was heading straight down the channel, trying to reach deeper water. Many tarpon fishermen anchor their boats and use buoys attached to their anchor lines to allow them to leave the hook and chase the fish. Drift fishing, I had the advantage of being able to follow the tarpon as it ran. Line poured from the rod as the fish tried to escape. Slowly, I tightened the drag enough to restrain the fish but not break the line. I felt the power of the fish as the bow of the boat turned and the tarpon pulled the boat forward.

A narrow opening in the mangroves appeared on my left, one I had never noticed before. The connection with nature was one of the things I liked about fishing. The focus provided by the hunt opened my eyes to things I would not have normally seen. The waning light gave no clue of the water depth, but I was determined to subdue my prey. The big three for fly fishermen are bonefish, permit, and tarpon. I had brought all but a tarpon to the boat and I wasn't planning on losing this one, but grounding my boat wasn't an option, either.

A hundred-pound fish doesn't tire easily, and with the current assisting him, the tarpon towed the boat toward the opening. There was no time to check the depth on the chartplotter or to find a satellite view on my phone. I had to make a decision now.

Standing in the bow, unable to see the electronics, I had nothing but my senses and accumulated knowledge to work with. Color was the best indicator of water depth: The old saying "brown, brown, run aground" is one of the first lessons that boaters in these waters learn. In the low light the water had turned black, but there appeared to be a good flow coming from the channel, a sign that there was a fair amount of water ahead.

Checking the drag every few seconds I let the fish pull me into the channel. Seeing several bends ahead, I was able to tighten the drag and retrieve some line. Suddenly the pull increased and I saw the water break as the fish leapt. Six feet of silver scales flashed as I leaned forward, bowing to the silver king, and allowing the fish some slack. My heart jumped into my throat as the line stretched to its breaking point. Time stopped as the tarpon reached the apex. In what seemed like slow motion, the fish re-entered the water and bolted for a small lagoon.

Finally, with enough water around me, I started to fight the fish. After pulling the boat through the channel the tarpon should have been exhausted, but several jumps in succession told me otherwise. The effort did take a toll, and I was able to gain line.

One more run as the boat drew closer did him in. As tired as the fish, I leaned against the gunwales grasping his upper lip between my fingers. I removed the hook and aligned his body with the current. At first he stayed still, but after a few seconds his tail fin started to twitch as the water running through his gills resuscitated him. When I felt a tug it was time. Gently, I released my grip, and watched my first tarpon swim away.

With my back to the leaning post, I drew several deep breaths, trying to bring my heart rate back to normal. As I relaxed, I looked around. It was almost dark; I'd been so focused on the fight I hadn't noticed. Now, inside a body of water I didn't know, I had a second of panic. Being on the water every day, I was attuned to the moon and tides, but that knowledge was of no use tonight. The sky was clear, but the moon wouldn't rise for several hours and when it did, it would be just the thin sliver of a crescent.

Removing the spotlight from the console, I plugged it into the cigarette lighter outlet and shot the beam ahead. I had gotten used to boating at night on open water, but between the confines of the lagoon and having to navigate the winding channel to reach Midnight Pass, I faced a challenge. The narrow beam showed my way ahead, but a boat was not a car; there were no brakes. Trying to find the sweet spot where I had enough speed to maintain steerage, but not enough to do any damage if I hit something, I spun the wheel and turned toward where I remembered the channel being.

Ahead was a small opening and I steered toward it. Moving the light between the mangroves ahead and the water below to check the depth, I saw something submerged dead ahead. Moving closer, I dropped to an idle and focused the beam into the water. The dark metal framework was hard to see, but the lobsters inside were clearly visible. As I swung the light around, the pen was easier to see. I had found what Scott was up to earlier.

Though I suspected they would officially be worthless, I used my personal phone to take pictures. Through its backup to the cloud, Martinez had access to my business phone, and this evidence was not something I was ready for him to see—not yet. I took as many pictures as I could to document the find, until darkness seemed to shrink the small lagoon, and I brought the light up to find my way out. Several missteps later I emerged into Midnight Pass and then the open bay.

Faster than I would have liked, the euphoria from the fight was over. The difficulty of navigating the dark waters at night and what I just had found weighed heavily on my mind. Arriving back at Adams Key, I docked and secured the boat. Taking my fly rod to the house, I hosed it off and leaned it against the Column, then headed upstairs to sort things out.

Checking my phone to see if there were any messages and to have a look at the pictures, I saw several texts. The usual "SUP?" from Allie, and a longer one from Justine that warranted an immediate reply. It was her first "official" day back after the murder, and in the course of processing the evidence she had found some information to share. I felt like a live wire stuck out here, my mind and body cranked up from the storm, Scott's visit, fighting the tarpon, and finding the lobster pen. I knew sleep was far off and texted Justine back, asking her if she was alright with me staying in Miami tonight.

The emojis said it all: clapping hands and a big smiley face. They did come with the condition that we would paddle together in the morning. Tossing a few things in my backpack, I locked up the house and went down to the boat. Thankfully Zero either didn't care or missed my exit, and I was soon motoring across the bay.

Looking like a delicate bowl holding the stars, the crescent moon cast just enough light to reveal the small waves. The swell from the storm had passed and the boat skipped across the water. My smile was back, if for nothing else than being able to see Justine.

Reaching headquarters, I checked that all the FWC boats were accounted for, then pulled into my slip and secured the center console. The tarpon had distracted me, but as I drove hunger started to envelop me. It had been a long time since my last meal and I pulled in to a grocery store where I bought bacon, eggs, and some other staples, figuring I would cook breakfast when Justine got home.

I realized I was exhausted too after I put the groceries away, and figured I would crash for a minute on the couch. My breakfast plan turned awry some time later, when I felt another body on top of mine. Through bleary eyes, I gazed at Justine's face directly above mine. Her body had me pinned and she apparently had other plans before breakfast. There was no fight from me—we would eat later.

I have to admit to falling asleep again and the faint glow of the predawn sky was breaking through the darkness when I finally woke.

"Breakfast?" I asked her.

"You bet. Worked up a bit of an appetite last night. Got some pent-up aggression there?" She punched my arm.

I swung my body and set my feet on the floor. "Lemme get some food going and I'll tell you the sordid details. You have some information, too?" I made a motion to lay back down, but was stopped by a pillow swung at my head.

"Daylight's burning. I want to get in a paddle before work."

I envied the simplicity of Justine's schedule: rise early, eat, paddle, eat, nap, work. Avoiding the pillow, I made my way to the bathroom, cleaned up, and moved on to breakfast. Standing at the stove, eggs and bacon to cook, I felt hands around my waist and the warmth of Justine's body against mine. I hated to kill the moment with work talk, but as she said, daylight was burning.

I explained what had happened yesterday.

"Ray? Really? But he's one of the good guys."

I knew what she meant. Without Ray's vigilance and work ethic the outer islands of the park, including the two campgrounds, would fall into disrepair. Sun, salt, rain, and heat didn't abide by schedules. The elements did everything in their power to thwart man's intrusion into the wilderness. I knew firsthand that Ray worked more than he reported, doing things when he knew they needed to be done, before nature had her way. Today, for example, I would bet he was already checking the campgrounds for damage from the storms.

"I guess you can be good and still break the law," I said.

"If that prick Martinez would pay you guys what you're worth, he wouldn't need to."

I hated to defend Martinez. His priorities were often questionable, but he did what every good government administrator did and spent his entire budget—needed or not—every year so as not to lose it the next. Unfortunately, our pay was above his own paygrade.

"What about your news?" I changed the subject.

"Right." She went back to the bedroom and returned with her phone. After a few swipes she handed it to me. "Scroll through them. *Vibrio* at its finest."

The Latin was my first clue; otherwise, I would have no idea what the tubular images in the pictures were. Thankfully, she embellished.

"Sid called and sent them over. Bacteria abide by their own rules and keep growing after the death of the victim. They're the culprits responsible for decomposition."

"From the wound?" I asked.

"Yup. It's called *Vibrio vulnificus*." The words rolled off her tongue without pause.

"Let me guess. From handling lobster?"

"Bingo, kemosabe. Not sure how he got it, though."

I had some idea. The process of detaching the tail from the body of the lobster is done by twisting them apart by hand. Even wearing gloves, on our best days when we harvested eight or so, I often ended up with puncture wounds from the sharp extrusions in the shell. Hence the name: spiny lobster. If my calculations were correct, Hayward was handling fifty or more bugs a day. Any one of them could have infected him. The question now was: What did this have to do with solving the case?

As usual, Justine provided the answer: "Any other guilty parties will have it, too."

13

STEVEN BECKER
A KURT HUNTER MYSTERY
BACKWATER FLATS

Before I could decide what to do with the information, my phone rang. It was about Martinez time and, with his multitude of tracking devices, I had to assume he knew where I was. Instead, after glancing at the phone, I saw it was Susan McLeash. Usually there'd have to be ice on the bay-waters before I'd want to talk to her, and I risked a quick glance at the weather screen before answering. Partly cloudy and eighty-eight degrees was the forecast, but I went ahead and accepted the call—this time I needed her.

"Well, good morning, sunshine," she started.

I might have wanted to talk to her, that didn't mean I had to like it.

"Susan."

There was a long pause while she figured out I wasn't rising to the bait.

"Hunter. I've made some progress with my assignment. If you're going to be down in this neck of the woods, maybe you could stop by and we can review."

It was all I could do to act civil after she referenced where I was. I'd gone as far as to buy a personal phone after Martinez's constant invasions of my privacy. Apparently having an adjacent office to Martinez was a good enough reason to share my location.

"Right. Should be down in an hour or so."

"Traffic depending." She laughed, and disconnected.

"Crap," I said, staring at the screen.

"Sounds like that was our girl?"

"The one and only. I've got to get going. Maybe this time she might have done something helpful. Thanks for the info on the bacteria." I wasn't sure how I was going to use it yet. Evidence from investigations tended to be random strands of information. You never knew which was going to be the one that solved the mystery.

It appeared that Susan was savvy to my route as well as my location. Her laugh made sense as red brake lights greeted me as I crept toward the merge on 836. A long thirty minutes later I had covered the five miles to the turnpike, where, driving opposite of the rush-hour flow, it became a speed-limit ride. Sitting in traffic, I had found it impossible to think, but once I started moving, so did my brain.

I had two assumptions I needed to confirm: Hayward was dirty, and Scott was clean. From our conversation and what seemed to be Scott's attempt to reintegrate the short lobsters back into the bay, he might even have been in the ultra-clean category. These types tended to be activists, so passionate about their fight they would often cross lines of legality. I was rooting against it, but it kept Scott near the top of my suspect list.

Exiting onto Palm Avenue, I headed east, continuing my train of thought. The first mile was the usual urban sprawl: stoplights and strip malls with cookie-cutter housing developments visible behind them. The next stretch was new construction, the previous pattern being repeated *ad nauseam*.

The construction suddenly ended and the dead-straight

road reverted to what I guessed was "natural" South Florida. Broken by intermittent pines, palms, and low brush, the vistas allowed by the flat terrain spread out for miles in front of me. I knew the Australian pines were invasive, as were the green and red iguanas sunning themselves beside the bumpy road, and the pythons hidden in the long grass beyond. As I turned toward headquarters, the road picked up a canal that ran alongside it. Every hundred yards or so, cars were pulled off to the side and I could see men and women fishing with cane poles.

Ten minutes later, I reached headquarters, still with as many questions as answers. Walking into the entrance, I saw Mariposa sitting behind the reception desk and decided, with Susan McLeash waiting upstairs, that procrastination was as good a tactic as any. Mariposa was my ally here, and we exchanged a few minutes of conversation, mostly my inquiring about her husband and his Appleton 21, "guest-only" rum, and she asking about Allie and Justine.

A figure appeared at the top of the stairs. Busted, I said goodbye to Mariposa and, with the body language of a death-row inmate, climbed toward Susan McLeash.

"Hunter. My office."

I shrugged and followed her. At least her office came before Martinez's. He probably knew where I was, but at least I didn't have to see him. Waiting for Susan to take her place behind the desk, I took the visitor's chair.

"You don't make friends easily, do you?" she asked.

I guessed who she was referring to. "Robinson?"

"Those guys want a piece of you."

"Ray, too." I hadn't meant to bring him into this, but hoped her influence with Robinson might take some heat off my neighbor.

Counting on her as an ally proved to be a mistake.

"It's not looking good for him. There'll probably be an official investigation."

I reminded myself to keep an open mind about my neighbor. "I'd like to solve a murder, not hang a co-worker."

"Right, clearance rates and all. Robinson sent over the personnel files for Hayward and Scott this morning. I reviewed them and found nothing untoward."

Leaving Susan to triage information was like jet skiers' penchants for jumping other boat's wakes. They thought it was fun, regardless of the safety of everyone else on the water. "I'd like to have a look anyway."

"Suit yourself. I'll email them to you."

"Any progress on the lobster release idea?"

"Actually, Robinson was receptive. Thought it could be good PR for the FWC and the park."

Or a smokescreen. "So, they haven't done anything along those lines? Did you find out what they've been doing with the shorts?"

When she leaned back and took a deep breath, my eye was drawn to the buttons on her shirt, which were stressed to the point of breaking. Thankfully she exhaled, saving the buttons and my eyes.

"So many questions," she said dismissively.

"If you could find out I'd really appreciate it." I rose to leave.

"Find out what?"

I walked out, then got an idea that I hoped she couldn't mangle. "Can you call the local clinics and hospitals and see if they've treated anyone with—" I had to look at the note I'd entered in my phone. Instead of trying to pronounce it, I copied and texted it to her. Waiting for her phone to ding, I was slightly disturbed to hear a duck quacking as her ringtone for me.

Picking up the phone, she read the message. "What's with that?"

"Bacteria. Anyone in contact with Hayward might have it."

"And you want to see if they sought treatment?"

That didn't deserve an answer, and I left for good. Faced with the decision of Martinez spotting me on the way to my office or escaping hell, I chose the latter. I wanted to see what Scott was up to, and also have a look at the lobster pen in the daylight. The tarpon in the pass would provide a good excuse for a stakeout.

On my way out of headquarters, I said goodbye to Mariposa, and walked to the docks. Mounted on a pole just below a security light, Martinez's camera caught my eye. Moving toward my boat, I noticed the FWC center console was gone. Another slip usually occupied by their twin-engine RHIB was empty as well, a very unusual occurrence.

As much as I hated to ask, I had to think that maybe enlisting Martinez's network of cameras might do some good. I might as well get some intel from his paranoia. Texting him rarely got a response, so I sucked it up and called. The request got a lukewarm response, but I could read between the lines and knew it was an act. If he could contribute to the investigation and get on the evening news, he would.

I asked him to check what time the boats had left and who their operators were, then disconnected. Hopefully, with Susan and Martinez occupied on small but potentially meaningful tasks, I hopped aboard my center console and headed out of the marina, ready to do some real detective work. Rounding the corner, I entered the channel and pulled across to the fuel dock. I was down about a half-tank, and with the dock empty, I idled toward the closest pump. Will met me and waited while I unscrewed the fuel cap before handing me the nozzle.

"On you or the company card?"

"This one's on the feds." I handed him the card, hoping Martinez wouldn't be distracted when the notification that I had spent some of his precious budget on gas crossed his screen. "Seen the FWC guys out here?"

"No, man, the dudes are out actually working since Hayward got killed. Even that fat-ass Robinson went out in the inflatable."

That explained why the RHIB was gone. I'd gotten information from Will before and decided to press. "You know where they're at?"

"Nah, I ain't exactly in the loop." He chuckled at his own joke. "Robinson looked hot, though. Pulled in for fuel. Dude was all edgy and shit. 'Bout bit my head off having to wait for a trawler to gas up in front of him."

I dug through my wallet, found a five, and thanked Will. He pocketed the bill and helped with the lines, then pushed the boat off the dock and into the channel.

At the entrance, I looked both ways to see if I could spot one of the FWC boats. If it had been one of the park-service craft like mine, Martinez would have the location, and I thought of asking if he could hack into the FWC computers and see if they tracked their boats as well, but figured one favor was enough for the day.

Thirty-five miles long and as wide as eight miles, the open spaces of Biscayne Bay were of little interest to people up to something.

That left the coast and out islands for nefarious activity. Whether you were committing a crime or preventing one, that's where the action was.

I already had seen Scott down by Midnight Pass. South of Turkey Point's grid of cooling canals, it was in a less-traveled area of the park. Smugglers chose the protection of the barrier islands; poachers seemed to like the mangrove-lined shores of the mainland. North of Bayfront Park and headquarters, I could see the Miami skyline through the haze. The waters from here to there were a lot busier than the southern part of the bay—which was the direction I turned.

It looked like a lot of water in front of me, but there were only two ways to reach the lagoon and the lobster pen. Following the coast would bring me in above the lagoon. The forest-green T-top would be visible from a distance if anyone was looking.

Instead, I chose to cross the bay and come in from below. I would have to fight a hundred feet of mangroves on foot, but I would reach the lagoon unobserved. As I steered toward Totten Key, I could see the markers for the channel leading to Card Sound ahead. Swinging around the red marker, I turned hard to the southwest and followed the channel, turning to the northwest after the last piling. I passed to the south of Long Arsenicker Key, being careful to avoid the shoals on its south side. Following the coast of the island, I crossed a skinny piece of water before coasting to a stop at a clump of mangroves that the chartplotter told me was the shortest route to the lagoon.

Using a dock line, I tied the boat off to a hefty mangrove branch and slid over the side. Swatting mosquitoes as I went, I struggled to keep my footing as I navigated the maze of roots, knowing that slipping off would find me knee-deep in muck. The lagoon was visible ahead, giving me hope that the chartplotter was correct, and a few minutes later, staying behind the last of the mangrove branches for cover, I had an unobstructed view of the lagoon.

Right over the pen were the two FWC boats.

14

SCOTT AND ROBINSON WERE ENGAGED IN A HEATED CONVERSATION —probably more of a fight. A strong breeze blew through the mangroves, making it impossible to hear what they were saying. This was a photo opportunity and, using my work phone, I snapped several pictures of the pair. Let Martinez see them together. Maybe then he would fork over more resources than his meager offer of computer assistance and Susan's supposed "cooperation".

A blue heron hunting nearby took flight after I stepped awkwardly on a branch, snapping it. I froze and checked the men on the water, but they appeared oblivious. Following the heron's lead, a flock of white ibis took to the skies. Using the disturbance to cover my movements, I crept closer to the lobster pen. Fifty feet away, I silently cursed the park service for choosing colors that attracted mosquitoes, but at least the forest green and khaki were perfect camouflage for the mangroves.

I could hear the men now.

"Our mandate does not include lobster nurseries," Robinson yelled at Scott.

"Beats the crap out of selling them. It's a preserve here.

Maybe we should protect it. You know—protect and serve," Scott countered.

I was starting to like Scott. It might not have been the FWC motto, but it sounded good. Robinson stood by the helm with one hand on the railing and the other on his hip. He easily absorbed Scott's tirade. His years of experience had taught him to let the storm blow over, but Scott baited him.

"I'll expose you. Hayward, too."

"You can't do shit to me. I'll have you reassigned to the Keys. See how you like that hell."

The Key's tagline is "fishing capital of the world," and it is. Spread out over a hundred twenty miles, the island chain, with a reef running parallel the entire distance, is impossible to police.

"Bullshit, what y'all were doing. This is damned near close enough to hell, working under you."

Robinson had heard enough. "I heard you were trouble. Consider yourself suspended pending further inquiry—without pay."

So Martinez-esque. The proclamation ended the conversation, and the two boats drifted apart. Scott waited for Robinson to leave before slamming his hands on the steering wheel. Stomping around the boat, he slapped the windshield with an open palm and proceeded to beat on the gunwales. Robinson's twin-engine boat had disappeared from view, leaving us alone. I wanted to call out and reassure Scott that I would have his back, but he was visibly disturbed and I didn't know how he would react to being spied on.

His tantrum over, he sat on the leaning post, staring into the water. Quiet once again settled over the lagoon. I was frozen like a statue. The heron, sensing the disturbance was over, returned to his fishing, and I waited to see what Scott would do. I could sympathize with his plight. More than once I had been accused of being holier than thou, although his behavior made my outbursts look small. As much as I felt akin to him, I had seen his violent streak. It might have been done in private, and we were all guilty of such behavior when we thought no one was looking, but I couldn't unsee it.

While I waited for him to make a move I thought about human nature. Every society had standards for conduct, but the lines were different for each person. I wondered if his anger was just enough to make him beat on a boat, or was there enough rage inside of him to kill a man?

It appeared that he had made a decision. Moving to the stern, he leaned into the water and reached down for what I guessed was a side panel of the pen. Regardless of what had happened, I believed his intentions were good—whether sanctioned or not. I didn't want him to abandon his efforts just because Robinson was an ass.

"Hey, Jim," I called out.

His head lifted and he looked around the lagoon. Realizing I was camouflaged by the mangroves, I stepped toward the water and called again.

"Oh, great. What are you doing here?"

The response was expected and thankfully not as defensive as I feared. "I can help."

"What, let the shorts go? Damned jewfish'll be snacking on them by dinner."

"No. I mean help keep your efforts alive."

His body visibly relaxed. I had his attention. "Hang on for a minute and let me bring my boat around."

"Whatever. If you heard Robinson, I've got nowhere I need to be."

"Yeah. It'll just take a few minutes." I stepped back into the mangroves and crossed to the bay side. The line I had tied to the branch was taut, the current having taken the boat to the extent of the restraint. Forced to wade the flat, I shuffled my feet to prevent sinking into the muck, as well as alerting any stingrays to my presence. Halfway to the boat, a pair of wakes spread out in front of me. Two bonefish. The elusive fish were taunting me, somehow knowing I didn't have a rod in hand. Watching them as they took off to deeper water, I reached the boat and climbed over the gunwale.

Without having to worry about being seen, I rounded Mangrove Point and entered the narrow channel leading to the lagoon. Scott remained as I had left him and I idled toward his boat. He made no move to put out fenders or offer a line. My presence, at least for now, had been accepted but was not welcome.

"Hey."

"How much of that did you see?" Scott asked.

"I heard most. Never did like that guy. Surprised he could even run a boat." That got a chuckle out of him.

"How'd you know we would be here?"

I told him about the tarpon dragging me into the lagoon last night and subsequently finding his nursery. "I actually asked Susan McLeash to talk to Robinson about setting up something like this."

"Well, looks like I have no choice but to take it down."

"I'll look after it for the time being." With the sun overhead, the setup was much easier to see than last night. About ten feet long and five wide, the metal panels that formed the side were constructed with openings large enough to allow baitfish and shrimp to get in, but too small for the lobster to escape."

"How long have you been doing this?"

"A while. With Hayward selling everything it was hard. On his days off I would tell Robinson there was no confiscated product, and put them here. I thought I could actually do some good until Robinson showed up this morning."

"Why not just release them near the park?"

"It's protected here and too shallow for the cubera snapper and jewfish to get at them. Nurse sharks'll get in here, that's why I have the pen. When they're bigger, I release them."

Though turtle rescue and release was a big deal, I wasn't sure lobsters would garner the same attention, but it was worth trying. "I'll have Susan talk to Robinson."

"Hmph. Those two scare the crap out of me."

It was my turn to smile. "She can be persuasive to a certain kind of guy." We both laughed. Things had lightened up enough that I thought I might ask him a favor. "Hey, my neighbor, Ray. Any chance you can back off him a little?"

His look changed. Whatever goodwill created at Susan's expense vanished.

"He's in violation," he said, then paused. "But I guess I'm suspended, so tell him to clean up his act and I'll back off."

His attitude confused me and I suspected I wasn't looking at an ally in this. I wasn't generally a *quid pro quo* kind of guy, and had been accused of enforcing rules too strictly. At least in my mind, there was a difference. When I chose to stand my ground, it was with a purpose, usually life safety. It sounds cliche, but I did draw a line. There were twenty-seven thousand pages of rules and laws. You had to choose which to enforce or you would get mired in detail and miss the big stuff that really mattered. Ray's side-business was probably a violation. But he wasn't hurting or taking advantage of anyone, besides maybe extricating a few dollars out of the commercial-fishing pot, but those guys were scared to fish that close to the park boundaries anyway.

I thought it better to drop it. "Right, I'll see what I can do with him. Appreciate it." While I waited for Scott to calm down I tried to think if there was another angle he could help with. At this point I had narrowed down my suspects to Hayward's buyers, a disgruntled fisherman, the man five feet from me, and

I hoped least likely, Ray. "You ever go with Hayward when he sold them?"

"Nah, and I didn't take any money, either. He tried to bring me in, but I flat-out refused."

"Why not turn him in?"

"Shit runs deep, man, and he knows my history. Threatened to tell the dudes I busted where they could find me." He looked away for a second.

I followed his gaze to the blue heron hunting on the other side of the lagoon and I wondered if he was trying to figure out how to check the bird's fishing license. At this point, I was wondering why it was Hayward in the morgue and not Scott. His holier-than-thou attitude was certainly abrasive.

"So, you went along with it?" I had my doubts he was capable of ignoring it.

He shrugged and turned back to watch the heron, ending our conversation. The bird, standing on one leg, recoiled, the feathers on its neck at attention, and stabbed its long beak into the water. With a twelve-inch fish struggling in its grasp, it looked up, opened its wings, and took off.

"I'll see what I can do about making this a permanent arrangement." I turned my gaze to the lobsters in the pen. When he didn't acknowledge me, I studied his expression. It looked like there was a bomb about to blow in him and I wasn't sure how long the fuse was. Without a word, he started his engine and idled away. I waited until he was around the first bend in the channel, and sat back trying to make sense of his anger.

I got it that Ray wasn't squeaky clean, but it wasn't the same as a dirty cop taking bribes to look the other way while people were killed. That might be a little melodramatic, but Ray busted his butt to keep the park running smoothly. If he needed to sell some legally caught seafood to make ends meet, that was more the fault of the government for not taking care of its own, not a crime. On the scale of poaching, he was small fish.

Movement in the pen caught my eye. The lobster had sensed some kind of danger and crept back into a corner. Looking around, I saw the shadow of a four-foot nurse shark as it passed over the bottom. Brushing against the metal grate, it felt for an entrance. Finding no way in, it moved on in search of easier prey. Watching the lobsters as they started to separate, sensing the threat was gone, something looked wrong to me.

Water distorts size by about twenty-five percent. I'd witnessed this first-hand when hunting for lobsters and spearfishing. It took a while to get a feel for a keeper, and those in the pen all looked legal. The water was shallow here, and I reached over the gunwale to try and extract one. The pen was crowded, making it easy enough, and I quickly had one in my grasp, but without a glove the sharp horns punctured my hands. Stepping back, I reached into the console, found a pair, and put them on. The little bit of protection allowed me to grab one of the smaller ones and I pulled it from the water.

I had no gauge on board, but did have a tape measure used for documenting crime scenes. Holding the crustacean in one hand, and, after fumbling to hook the end over the carapace, I pulled the tape to the end. It showed three and a quarter inches. Considerably larger than the three-inch limit.

15

STEVEN BECKER
A KURT HUNTER MYSTERY
BACKWATER FLATS

I checked a half-dozen, each time with the same result. There was no question, that the lobster were legal. I had to assume my tape measure was accurate, leaving the gauge used to measure them suspect—and the possible murder weapon.

Lobster gauges are simple instruments. Since they are made from lightweight metal or plastic, it's easy to make a homemade version. I didn't recall any writing on any of them, either: There was no information from a manufacturer, or a logo, or even an identifier like "Lobster Gauge." Untraceable: Gauges could come from anywhere.

Finding legal-sized lobsters here complicated things further. The potential markets for the lobsters was wide open now. I was no longer looking for someone willing to buy shorts "off the books." To complicate things further, if Hayward had a shill with a commercial license, the tails could be sold to any of hundreds of distributors or seafood operations, including mom and pop shops, and restaurants.

My next steps were clear: First, find the "fixed" gauge used to incorrectly measure the lobsters, and then find out who was buying them. Locating the gauge, which was also possibly the murder weapon, was my first priority; I already had a good idea who I could talk to about the market, especially if Hayward was selling them without a license.

Before I left, I realized that, although I'd taken pictures with my personal cell, I hadn't adequately documented the pen or my discovery of the lobster inside it with my work phone. Martinez would see the pictures as they uploaded to our cloud storage, and they would also be GPS-stamped for location, as well as time and day.

Satisfied the pictures were clear enough, I pulled several lobsters out of the pen. It was a bit of a struggle to hold the tape measure and take pictures at the same time. My solution was to place the hooked metal end of the tape measure in the closed cooler top and, using the three-to-six-inch marks, I could hold the crustaceanary evidence in one hand and the phone in the other. They weren't perfect, and the angle I had taken the photos from was not clear enough for them to be used as evidence, but they were good enough to prove my theory.

When I had finished with the scene, I looked around the lagoon one more time and, finding nothing of importance, decided to leave. It was easier locating the channel in the daylight than it had been last night, and as I idled through the winding passage, I started thinking. Finding the rigged gauge would be essential, but I decided to try my other investigative option first to both save some miles and to talk to Ray. Calling him on the radio might attract unknown and unwanted attention, so texted him. At least I would know who was (and wasn't) listening in. It wasn't unusual for me to communicate during the day with Ray. I often saw things while out on patrol that Martinez missed with his desk-bound surveillance.

He responded that he was on Boca Chita Key, working on the docks there. The island was near the northern border of the park, miles past headquarters. Changing my plan, I texted that I would catch him later, and headed toward Bayfront Park.

Whatever weather had blown through last night was long gone, leaving in its wake a comfortable day. That description was a bit of a misnomer in the land where five months of the year could be classified as "hell." Today didn't rank as one of those and, despite my churning mind, I enjoyed the ride across the bay. Having my conscious thought occupied with piloting the boat had freed my subconscious to sort things out. Investigating a murder isn't philosophical. The journey is not the destination—only a solution is. As I pulled into my slip, I had no answers, but at least I had a plan.

Looking around the marina I saw the twin-engine RHIB that Robinson had used earlier. There was no point in checking it for evidence. Robinson was the sole user of the vessel and I doubted he would have killed a co-conspirator on it. Not one to get his hands dirty, his involvement probably amounted to receiving a fat envelope for his sanction. The single-engine FWC boat wasn't there either, and I wondered where Scott had gone after leaving the lagoon. In retrospect, I should have followed him. The evidence would have been there when I returned.

With no other options, I turned to the two-story headquarters building to see if Martinez could help. That thought alone dropped my mood into the depression zone. Trying to get over it, I did what all the feel-good experts advise: put a smile on—even if it's fake. But faking it was a wasted effort, as seeing Mariposa brought the real thing to my face.

I gave her my usual shrugged-shoulder greeting.

She knew the question. "Seems like he's in a pretty good mood today, Kurt," she said with her sing-song island accent.

"That's a first."

"Him and Susan are cooking something up. Maybe better watch yourself."

"I'll do that."

"Hey. I sent my husband out to buy another bottle of Appleton 21. I think he'll be wanting someone to drink with. Saturday night?"

I was about to jump at the invite, then realized Allie and her friend would be here. "I've got Allie this weekend, and she's bringing a friend."

"The more the better."

"You're sure?" I wasn't going to impose two teenagers on anyone—but the rum....

"No problems, me and Justine will take good care of them."

I accepted, then realized my error and texted the boss to confirm. Thankfully, Justine returned the question with a smiley face. Counting those hours as time off from entertaining two teenage girls, I again smiled as I walked upstairs to the offices.

Martinez's door was partially open, with only the legs of the empty visitor's chair that Susan usually occupied visible. The steel door jamb made a hollow sound when I rapped my knuckles on it, and I was told to enter—of course he knew who it was.

"Hunter. Surprised to see you so soon after your last visit."

"Did you see the pictures I took earlier?"

"I did. Not sure nature pictures are part of your scope of work—or is spying on another department."

Leaving out the part about the tarpon leading me there, I explained about how I had found the lobster pen and the encounter between Robinson and Scott this morning.

"That's all very interesting."

True to his administrator's DNA, he failed to understand the importance of what I found. "Any chance you were able to track the FWC boats?"

"You want to know where Scott is? Look up the DSC

number." He must have seen the confused look on my face, and continued. "Really, Hunter. Do you even read my emails?"

"I noticed the new radio." I knew DSC, or digital select calling, had been implemented on our boats. Remaining quiet, I waited for his lecture without admitting my ignorance.

"Each vessel has an MMSI, or maritime mobile service identity, number. By inputting the FWC boat's number into your radio, provided their radio is on, you'll be able to contact the operator privately and exchange positions."

"But he'll know I'm looking for him."

"So, make something up. Just get him to answer your call."

"How do I find the number?"

"Really, Hunter. Who's the investigator here?" He turned to his computer, and moved through several screens. The Darth Vader ringtone I had assigned him went off, indicating the receipt of a message, a split second after he turned back to me. Waiting for a reprisal I held my breath. I usually silence the device before meetings, but had forgotten. He seemed to be either ignorant of the ringtone, or enjoyed it. Either way it was hard to tell from his stone face.

"Go ahead and look. I just sent the entire FWC directory to you."

Checking my phone, I scanned through the spreadsheet. Sorting by location, I selected Biscayne National Park, and waited for the results to filter. Three entries remained, but the individual boats were only labeled by registration numbers. Looking out the window, I checked the RHIB and copied the other two numbers to a memo. "Appreciate your help." I turned to leave, but then thought about Susan. "Any idea if Susan's had any luck with Robinson?"

"They're out to lunch as we speak."

That explained Robinson's hasty exit earlier. "Lunch" with those two could easily turn into happy hour and then ... I tried to erase the visual from my mind. That probably meant the assignment I'd left for her was un-done as well.

"She was going to call around to the urgent care facilities and emergency rooms about an infection that was found in Hayward's wound. Mind if I ask Mariposa to help out?"

He pursed his lips. "Go ahead." He turned back to his trio of monitors, dismissing me.

I was starting to reach critical mass with my situation here and did my best to hold my temper. It had seemed like a lifeline when I was transferred here two years ago. My ex, Jane, had already been awarded sole custody and had taken Allie to her sister's in Palm Beach County. I figured they'd be safe there after the cartel firebombed our home out west. It was me the bad guys were after and being offered the job at Biscayne, an out-of-the-way park thousands of miles away, took the pressure off me personally. Over the past year my family life had normalized as much as Jane and our divorce would allow.

The job had taken some getting used to. Moving to Adams Key and spending most of my time on the water was a big change, but I'd quickly settled into island life. Running the boat took a bit longer to master, but I now felt confident in that regard as well. Now, after solving a half-dozen high-profile cases as well as handling the run of the mill stuff, it was time to sort out my professional life. That meant I needed to put my foot down with Martinez and Susan McLeash. I had been their doormat for the last two years and was over it.

On the way out, I asked Mariposa to call around about the infection. She was sweet about accepting the assignment, probably knowing why I'd asked her. I left the building feeling defeated.

Heading back to the marina, I saw no sign of Scott's boat, so I climbed aboard mine and pulled up the memo on my phone. Turning on the VHF radio, I scrolled through the menus until I saw the screen to enter an MMSI number. The nine-digit number punched in, I hit the call key and waited.

It was protocol for all government, as well as commercial and recreational boaters, to monitor channel 16. If Scott was on the water, his radio should be on. A few seconds later, my radio beeped and I shielded the display from the sun. There was no answer, but a set of coordinates displayed on the screen. In an effort to enhance his surveillance scheme, Martinez might have sprung for upgrades to our radios, but there was no direct interface with the chartplotter. I entered the latitude and longitude manually, checking each set of numbers as I went, then hit GOTO.

Extending past the edge of the chartplotter's screen, a dark pink line displayed the route to Scott's boat. I had to zoom out several times to see his location. Not being able to distinguish hazards, the line ran straight through Turkey Point's cooling canals, and exited into the bay near Mangrove Point. Zooming out one more time, I saw the destination was the lagoon.

The feeling I had, that I should have followed Scott earlier returned.

16

Frustrated by my encounter with Martinez, I ran the boat harder than the conditions allowed. With every wave, spray flew over the bow, covering me in seawater. The fifteen-knot southerly wind meant the typically calm water was covered in whitecaps, and to make matters worse my course took me directly into them. I had started to shiver well before I reached the lagoon. You wouldn't think a person could get cold in eighty-plus degree weather but, between the spray hitting me and the wind combined with the boat speed, I was chilled to the bone.

I thought about calling for backup, but there was really no one besides Johnny Wells, my buddy with ICE. The bay wasn't his area, but I suspected he would help if I asked. Unfortunately, his Interceptor hadn't been in the marina, taking him out of play. As I approached, I felt a sinking feeling in my gut. There was nothing good going on in the lagoon, and I was going in alone. I thought about sending a text to Justine so someone would know where I was headed, but decided against alarming her.

Mangrove Point was coming up on my starboard side. Before entering the pass, I slowed enough to remove my sidearm from the glove box, where I kept it while on the water to protect it from the elements, and to check the shotgun, stored in the console. Removing that weapon from the securing clips, I checked the chamber and magazine. I liked to leave a uncocked, as just the sound of it sliding into the chamber was often enough of a deterrent.

Ready as I was ever going to be, I idled into the pass. I stopped briefly at the entrance to the channel leading to the lagoon and listened for a minute. The waves breaking against the hull and shore were the only sounds I heard, but that meant little. When the water is kicked up by the wind, as now, it is surprisingly loud. Anything short of a gunshot would be inaudible.

My senses were on high as I entered the channel. As the lagoon spread out before me, I breathed a sigh of relief when I saw nothing there. Nothing. Glancing around, I noticed the exposed mangrove roots. The tide was low enough that the top of the lobster pen should have been visible, but from where I sat there was no evidence of it. Idling over to its location, I peered into the green water. With the wind blowing, even the protected waters of the lagoon were murky, making it impossible to see the bottom.

There was only one way to find out for sure. Stripping my shirt off, I emptied my pockets, grabbed a mask from the console, and slipped over the side. I dropped under the surface, and started stroking around the area. I submerged several times and combed the bottom, although I was barely able to see my extended hand, .

There was no sign of the pen.

Returning to the boat, several possibilities ran through my mind and I settled on three scenarios: Scott had taken it down, Robinson had taken it down, or a boat had run over it and collapsed it. I decided to discard option three, as there were no other boats out. I was left with Scott or Robinson being the culprit. The DSC locator on Scott's boat had brought me here, making him the likely option—but why? Just as I started to ponder the possibilities, my phone vibrated. The screen showed the call was from a local number, but not one in my contacts. Bracing myself for a telemarketer, I answered, surprised when it was Robinson on the other end.

"Scott took off with one of the FWC boats."

I asked the obvious: "How does this concern me?"

"Stolen boats in the park would fall under your purview."

That set me back a step. I feigned like I hadn't overheard their earlier fight. "You'll have to explain."

"Do I need to call that dickhead boss of yours?"

At least we agreed on something. "Where are you? I'd be happy to meet and get the details."

"I'm standing in the marina at your freakin' headquarters staring at the empty slip my boat is supposed to be in."

There was nothing to be gained from staying here, and I had an idea, one that Martinez might actually help with. "I'll be there in thirty minutes."

It had taken me closer to forty-five to get down here, but with the wind and seas behind me, and being already wet, it would be a faster ride back. After my boss's latest blowup about messing with the internal affairs of the FWC, I thought it might be better to drag Robinson up to Martinez's office to review the footage, rather than ask over the phone.

A half-hour later, I stopped just outside of the channel and put my shirt back on. From the marina's entrance I could see Robinson pacing the dock. Pulling past the twin-engine RHIB, I noticed the empty slip where the center console Scott had been using usually docked. With a larger-than-usual snarl on his face, the FWC boss came toward my slip. He stopped short of helping and stood with his arms crossed while I tied off the boat.

"Well?" he huffed.

After Martinez's constant warnings about meddling in other agencies' affairs, I had to make sure this was by the book. Reaching into the console, I grabbed my clipboard, stocked with incident reports. Whatever I did would be documented and legal.

"A freakin' report? You're going to make me fill out paperwork?"

Reaching into my pocket, I removed a pen and started writing. Reluctantly, Robinson answered the questions. To my surprise, he was pretty honest about the incident this morning. There was no talk of the lobsters or the pen, but he was clear that he had suspended Scott several hours ago. The boat, with Scott in it, was well overdue.

"Can we talk about Hayward's murder?"

"How the hell is that related to my missing boat?"

"I'll find your boat, but something bigger is going on here."

"Do your job, Hunter. Find the boat!" He turned and walked away.

I figured Scott was smart enough to turn off his radio if he was on the run, and so I wasn't disappointed when I couldn't locate him through my VHF. That left me to use Martinez and his resources, as well as begging a question: Why didn't Robinson locate the boat through his own network?

That question was also the first thing out of Martinez's mouth when I handed him the incident report. Robinson had failed to sign it, but I knew Martinez had been watching—his office, as well as his cameras, overlooked the docks.

"I don't know what his game is, but somehow this is related to Hayward's murder. But you warned me about not getting up in another department's business."

He waved me off, as if to dismiss me, but still holding the original incident report. He now owned a piece of paper that would justify his actions. "I'll do some digging on my end. Did Susan speak to him?"

That was a good question. "I thought she was seeing him today?"

We looked at each other. "Get on it, Hunter. We have a missing agent."

I took that as permission to do my job—something that wasn't often granted outright from him. Executing a hasty exit so as not to allow him time to change his mind, I briefly stopped to chat with Mariposa and see if she'd had any luck with the clinics and hospitals. She had called as I asked, but the responses were all negative. I wondered if we shouldn't broaden our search to include Miami, but with the recent developments, I didn't think it would be worthwhile. I certainly wasn't going to give her busywork.

While Martinez checked his footage, I figured a run across the bay, some lunch, and a change of clothes were in order. Sometimes, given a little space, things often resolve themselves. With Susan (I hoped) having lunch with Robinson, I knew where two of the three parties were. Scott was missing, but he had not been gone long enough to warrant an all-out search. Figuring another hour wouldn't hurt anything, I started up the boat and left the marina.

Crossing the bay, I remembered my prior to-do list. Finding the lobster buyer might give the defining answer, and I hoped Ray was around to answer some questions on that subject. I also needed to pass on Scott's threat and ask my neighbor how he sold his product.

It was a slow ride home. The wind had increased a few knots since the morning and, looking behind me, the sky showed signs of storms forming over the mainland. Those often extinguished themselves before reaching open water, but—if this was even possible—the air felt more humid than usual. I suspected we might be in for another squally afternoon. That, at least, might separate me from the political maneuvering on the mainland, and give me a little time to figure some things out.

I was wrong on all counts. Adams Key came into view and I pushed down on the throttle, then saw both the FWC center console and Ray's boat at the dock. I had solved the case of the missing agent, but I feared for my neighbor.

Spray flew over the port rail as I pushed the boat hard through the side chop. It turned out to be a wasted effort. From a hundred yards away I could see a man and woman sitting in the FWC boat. Ray was nowhere in sight as I dropped to an idle and pulled up behind the center console. Scott, unlike his boss, came over to help with the lines. Susan McLeash didn't.

The two of them were an odd couple. I could tell by their body language—the way they didn't look at each other and the distance they kept between them, even when sitting on the boat —that they weren't happy to be together.

"Robinson is looking for you. Might be a good idea to tell him when you'll be back with the boat." I had thought about offering to cover for him, but with Susan here that wasn't a good idea.

"Hello, Susan," I started, having no idea why she was here or what she wanted from me. She was supposed to be having lunch with Robinson. I doubted her reason would include an offer to help.

"Okay, Hunter," she said, crossing her arms. "Robinson was all pissy and wanted nothing to do with the idea when I called him. He even canceled our lunch date."

With a pouty look on her face that threatened to crack her makeup, which had already taken a beating on the boat ride out here, she paused.

"Anyway, I've heard rumors that 'ol Jim Scott here might be receptive. He told me he was suspended this morning and I thought maybe you could help out. It is your *little* project that got him in trouble."

I looked over at Scott. We both knew this wasn't entirely true, but I didn't want Susan involved. Casting him a warning look that I hoped she wouldn't catch, I turned back to her.

"So, how did you two lovebirds get together?" I was trying to assemble a timeline of Scott's activities since the fight with Robinson.

"Funny, Hunter. I called Jim and he asked me to meet him at the dock by Turkey Point. He sounded excited about the idea. I didn't think there was any risk until he dragged me out here. I'm guessing it was a ruse to get me here. Now, *you're* going to take me back." She uncrossed her arms, climbed to the dock, walked to my boat, stepped down to the deck, and settled herself onto the leaning post.

"You're the only one that can help me," Scott said

"Then why take Susan? I would have met you if you called."

"Has to be under the radar, and this one is mixed up with Robinson and Hayward. Thought it might be a good idea to take her out of play." He motioned to Susan.

"Mixed up like a gin and tonic. We just go for drinks and hang out!" Susan yelled.

I gave her a look that commanded her to settle down. "Let me get a change of clothes and I'll run you back to your truck," I added to make sure she got the point, then turned toward my house.

Before I even made it off the dock, I heard Ray's screen door open. Zero, seeing fresh blood, bolted down the stairs, but skidded to a stop ten feet away from Susan. I had to give it to the dog; he knew how to pick his friends. Beer in hand, Ray followed behind him and headed straight for Scott.

"What the hell are you doing out here?" He set the bottle down on the dock and approached the FWC boat.

I sensed what was coming and moved to intercept him, but Zero decided to get in on the action and pushed me out of the way. As he moved to Ray's side, he started growling at Scott. Ray stepped into the boat and quickly moved toward Scott. I jumped in, landing in the bow, and quickly made my way around the console to break up the two men.

17

STEVEN BECKER
A KURT HUNTER MYSTERY
BACKWATER FLATS

I was a step faster getting to Ray than his first punch was getting to Scott. I hoped I'd stopped things in time that Scott wouldn't press charges. Separating the two men, I pulled Ray toward the bow.

"Not the way to get this done," I said, getting right in his face.

"Shit, Kurt. He's messing with my family."

In an indirect way Ray was right, but my friend also was using family to justify doing something illegal, if only slightly so, at least in my opinion.

"Go back up. I'll get rid of him." I shot a look in Scott's direction. "We'll talk later."

Ray left with a *humph* and several not-so-veiled threats. Zero followed. When he reached the steps to his house, I drew a deep breath. Moving to get off the boat, I paused by the console, where several lobster gauges were clipped to the T-top support. It was hard to tell from a quick glance if they were the doctored ones used to confiscate legal lobsters from the boaters who the FWC officers stopped, or if one happened to be the murder weapon, but I was not going to give up the chance to find out.

"Susan!" I called over to my boat. "Take my boat. I'll take Scott back." I figured that would separate them, as well as remove any chance of Scott making a run for it. Scott moved back to the leaning post. After his suspension, then his run-in with Ray, and now being relieved of his craft, he wasn't a happy guy, but at least I wasn't arresting him. I'd witnessed his temper already, and though I didn't expect trouble from him now, I left him sitting there with a cross look on his face.

Susan, about to drive off in my boat, had several incidents with firearms on her record. I couldn't imagine how she could possibly get into trouble by herself, but this craft and any weapons on it were my responsibility.

Moving past her, I pulled my pistol from the glove compartment and buckled the gun belt around my waist. Out of habit I checked to make sure my handcuffs were in the small pouch, just in case I needed to subdue Scott. I took the key to the console from the chain and locked the compartment with the shotgun inside, then pocketed the key. I suspected there were weapons aboard the FWC boat as well. I would keep an eye on Scott. Truthfully, I was worried more about Susan taking my boat than having any problems with Scott.

With the case of the rogue agent and missing boat solved, we set off across the bay. For once I was grateful for the engine noise, which was loud enough to make conversation difficult. Twenty minutes later, with Susan following somewhere behind me, I entered the channel leading to the marina next to headquarters and pulled the boat into its slip. Martinez and Robinson were standing on the dock looking like Laurel and Hardy. I wasn't sure how, but Susan must have informed Martinez that we were headed this way.

I could feel Scott tense beside me as the pair walked toward the boat.

"Your suspension has now become a termination. I'll expect all your gear in my office before close of business today," Robinson said.

Even Martinez was surprised. Firing a government employee was not easy, and returning a boat a few hours late was far from cause. I had no intention of intervening and, for once, took Martinez's advice from earlier this morning. After securing the lines by myself, I pulled the key and kill switch from the ignition panel.

Robinson and Martinez were focused on Scott. Susan was as aggressive running a boat as she was everything else. Unsafe at any speed was a good description, but the same conditions that had threatened to streak her makeup had slowed her down. With Susan yet to arrive, and the three men staring at each other, I saw my opportunity and grabbed the gauges from where they were clipped to a horizontal rail on the T-top. Stashing them in the large outer pocket of my cargo shorts, I stepped onto the dock. Handing the keys to Robinson, I walked toward my slip to wait for Susan.

I heard the engine before I saw my boat, and breathed a sigh of relief as it entered the marina. In addition to her tendency to shoot guns that weren't hers at inopportune times, Susan had a reputation for being a reckless boater. She approached the slip too fast and, unable to do anything, I watched her come in hot. Too late, she dropped into neutral, but I was able to fend the boat off the dock with my foot. Rather than watch her fumble around trying to dock against the wind and current, I stepped aboard. She readily relinquished control and I eased the boat into the dock. To her credit, she helped with the lines.

"I'll give you a ride to your truck," I said quietly, not wanting Robinson or Martinez to hear. The former was watching Scott as he removed his personal items from the boat; the latter had disappeared. Not wanting to give her a chance to talk to either man, I started walking toward the parking lot.

"Slow down. I want to hear what's going on."

Without turning or slowing down I called back to her: "I'll tell you all about it on the ride over." That seemed to satisfy her, and she double-timed it to my truck. I unlocked it, started the engine and powered down the windows at the same time as I turned the AC to max. It wasn't all that hot out, the day not even registering on the "hell" scale, but the subtropical sun had turned the truck into an oven. I waited for Susan to get in the passenger side, and started out of the lot.

We drove in silence, letting the combination of the open windows and air conditioning cool the interior to a tolerable level. When I finally felt the cool air win, I closed the windows and told Susan everything that had happened today, leaving out the gauges and my theory about them. I wanted her to hear the details from me and not cobble together her own version. Given the chance to speculate, she would go running to Martinez and Robinson, like a high-school girl with two dates to the prom.

"Robinson can't fire Scott for that," she said, when I finished.

"I don't know if there's other stuff. He's passionate about his work, I'll say that for him."

"Dudley Do Right, they call him."

Of course, Susan was privy to the gossip. "What else do they say?" I tried to keep her talking.

"The usual."

As a government employee, I had a pretty good idea what she was referring to. People in the private sector often seek out government jobs, knowing the conditions and benefits are superior. The pay was often lower, though not by much, but adding in the benefits of health insurance and a pension plan, which the government provides, it didn't take a master's degree to tell you which kind of job was more secure. Those who had never worked on the outside, and those who had and forgot, convinced themselves they were getting a raw deal. My dad had been a contractor and had encouraged me to follow in his footsteps, offering me his business when he retired. I'd done it for a while, but we couldn't get along. I remembered well how hard it was. If I counted all the hours he worked when I was growing up, I wasn't sure he even made minimum wage. Susan had never worked for anyone beside the park service. She had no idea.

"Any of them throw around money?"

"Kurt."

I glanced over at her and immediately turned away, wishing I hadn't. She looked like a sixth-grader pouting.

"I just go for drinks once in a while. It's happy hour, you know, two for one."

I couldn't hold it against her that she only saw what she wanted to. Her priority was getting free drinks, not scoping out the agents. None made enough money to be boyfriend material.

"Just asking. You think you can find out what Robinson's got to say later?"

I swear she winked. "Now, that's my kind of assignment."

The landscaped entrance to the Turkey Point power plant stood out as an oasis amongst the scrub, brush, and canals. Once inside the property, I couldn't wait to discharge my passenger. I dropped her at her truck and pulled away without waiting for her to unlock the door. After fifteen minutes alone with Susan McLeash, I felt like I needed a shower.

Aside from Susan irritating me, the lobster gauges in my cargo pocket had been poking my thigh. I hadn't wanted to remove them with her in the truck, but now, I slowed and pulled them out. I badly wanted to get them to Justine but, with my current shaky standing with Miami-Dade, I had to follow protocol. I liked to think their requirement for a case number, which meant the department knew who to bill for the work, was merely good practice, not anything against me personally, but I knew otherwise.

When I first arrived here, Justine had the run of the old lab. Working the swing shift allowed her freedom to work alone. The aged facility had been the incubator for our relationship. Without having to worry about anyone watching, she had often helped me with cases, many times with me looking over her shoulder. That had all changed when the new, state-of-the-art lab was opened last year. To mitigate or justify the cost, or maybe both, the techs needed to log their hours with each piece of equipment to a specific case. I supposed it was good business, but that didn't do much for me personally. With the closing of the old lab, we had lost our freedom. Except for late at night—or early morning, depending on your perspective—there were usually other techs around, and when they weren't, there were cameras positioned to observe the entire area.

Detective Grace Herrera once had been my connection with Miami-Dade. She had a way of staying above the fray and not allowing the petty political machinations of the department to influence her. For her effort, she was given a well-deserved promotion, but her rise in the department had left me in the cold. Now, it was Martinez who had to authorize the work. I didn't expect he was happy with the FWC after tying up his resources for the afternoon and, hoping my conduct today had put me in his good graces at least temporarily, I pulled out my cell, pressed his name in my contact list, and hit connect.

Whether he knew it or not, I was already heading to Miami and there was no way to obfuscate the road noise, anyway. So, I just told him what I had found and where I was headed. To my surprise, he said he'd file the paperwork. Now, I just had to clear it with the real boss—Justine.

She sounded excited and there wasn't even a dead body involved. Several minutes later, she called back with the green light for me to come by. All the dominos were falling in place, and I must have subconsciously accelerated, as seconds later I had to brake hard and veer onto the shoulder to avoid the car in front of me. Taking a deep breath, I pulled back into the bumper-to-bumper turnpike traffic. Martinez and the powers that be were working in my favor. The Miami traffic wasn't.

18

STEVEN BECKER
A KURT HUNTER MYSTERY
BACKWATER FLATS

The exterior doors of the building that housed the lab were still open, and I crossed the lobby and waited for Justine to let me in the interior security door. It took her several minutes to get there and in the interim several workers left through the magic door, each one eyeing me suspiciously. I didn't recognize them, but I suspected my picture was posted on the wall in the break room with the caption, "Don't do him any favors" below it.

Finally, I saw her and, regardless of the circumstances, my heart leapt. I wasn't sure how long the honeymoon phase lasted, but we were still in ours. She pulled the door open and held it, while even the automatic closer tried to deny my entrance. I slipped in anyway. Passing the stairs that led down to the old lab, we entered the new annex. Floor-to-ceiling glass on both sides of the hall protected the inner workings of the Miami-Dade forensics lab. Beyond the barrier, individual LED lights glowed from the pieces of equipment set in orderly rows. It was past six, and there were only a few desk-lights showing the occupied workstations.

"What do you have for me?" she asked, pulling me around the corner and planting a big kiss on me.

Anxious that we would be seen, and really missing the old lab, I pecked her cheek back. We entered the lab and I pulled the gauges from my pocket, handing them to her. Her brows furrowed, and she kind of cocked one eye half-closed. I knew I was in trouble and, wanting to avoid the lecture, started to explain. "My prints and DNA are going to be all over them."

"Evidence bags. Gloves. Hello..."

"I grabbed them on the run. I should have bagged them when I got to the truck, but they haven't left my pocket."

She rolled her eyes. This argument wasn't over, but the gauges drew her attention. "So, what's up with these?"

"Sid said he thought a metal gauge like this could have killed Hayward."

"And there are thousands of these suckers between here and Key West. What makes you think these are special?"

"I'll bet they are."

Gauges in hand, she took them to a table with a large light illuminating the surface. A pistol, a few casings, and some other evidence were quickly placed in a cardboard box and set aside. I remained silent as she got to work. Justine had her own process, and I figured if I was patient and let her work through it, the results would be the same, and it would be better for our marriage.

Her first step was to lay the gauges on a piece of black felt to provide contrast. Pulling a camera out, she took several pictures of them, then laid a ruler next to them and took several more. I waited, holding my breath for her to discover what I suspected.

"Hey, they're over three inches."

The ruler showed a strong eighth of an inch over—maybe more. From my experience, the majority of the crustaceans fell in this range, maximizing the officers' take without being too obvious.

She realigned the ruler for a more accurate measurement. "Three and a quarter? You got these off the FWC boat?"

I nodded and explained everything that had happened over the last few days.

"They've been fleecing the public for their own gain." She was angry now.

Revealing the entire scam, I explained how they set up what amounted to a roadblock near the ramp, checked boaters as they came in, and issued warnings about the confiscated product while writing tickets for safety infractions.

"The boaters are thinking they got off easy. They'll never report the officers taking their lobster."

"Exactly. But the trail ends there."

Having taken proper precautions from the moment she grabbed them, she already had a pair of nitrile gloves on, and picked up one of the gauges. Swinging a magnifying glass over the object, she turned on the unit's light and started to examine the gauge. "I'm not seeing anything unusual."

"Try the other."

She swapped gauges and started inspecting the second. Seconds later, she turned to me. "I've got blood."

Leaning over her, I saw the faint trail on the edge of the blade. "Could be from a fish, or a cut, or something.

"See this?" She showed me a knot of hair. "That doesn't look like it came from a fish. You may have found the murder weapon."

"What's next?" It felt good to be finally getting somewhere. Really good, but I didn't want to jinx it, and kept my poker face intact

"Oh, I've got a busy night ahead with this."

She liked to work alone and that sounded like my signal to get lost.

"Breakfast later?" Turning back to her workstation and

ignoring me, she confirmed my suspicion by not responding to the question. I'd been around her long enough that her obsession with her work didn't bother me; rather, it defined her—that and several other lovable qualities.

Leaving the lab, I glanced back, but she was too involved in whatever test she was running to notice. It was just getting dark when I stepped outside and wondered what to do. There was no way I could sit around the condo or head back to the isolation of Adams Key when I knew her results were only hours away. I thought about Susan, wondering if something might be gained by finding her happy-hour spot.

Scott might have known where it was, but I didn't want to involve him any further. The man's career was already in the proverbial chum-grinder. Mariposa seemed to know more about the goings-on at headquarters than anyone, and even though the FWC wasn't based there, their officers were around often enough that she had probably chatted them up. In any case, I knew if I asked her anything, it would be held in confidence.

The conversation started with some stilted pleasantries. I hadn't wanted to call her when she was off-duty. Mariposa has a knack for getting to the heart of the matter. She saw through my pretense, and allowed the conversation to shift to work, and told me about two bars. One in Cutler Bay, the other in Kendall, where she suspected they hung out. Thanking her and again confirming we would be over Saturday night, I punched the name of the closer place in my phone and headed to Kendall.

It was a strip-mall affair, but a chain, and it didn't look like a dive, either. Entering, I saw a myriad of TVs lining the walls and set over the bar. I scanned the crowd and saw no one familiar. I thought about asking the bartender, but decided against it. If they did hang out here, he might contact one of the officers and let them know that someone was asking questions. Catching a look at myself in a mirror, I didn't expect the uniform would do me any good, either, and when I got back to the truck, I changed into a polo shirt. The khaki shorts were vanilla enough; I didn't think anyone would notice they were federal-issue.

Cutler Bay was the next stop, and in the same kind of establishment, I scored. The problem now was how to infiltrate a group where I probably wasn't welcome. My tactic was to ignore them. Walking directly to the bar, I sat by myself and asked the bartender for a beer. I didn't necessarily want to drink it, but ordering a non-alcoholic beverage would be just lame. I could see the reflection of the group on one of the flat-screen TVs set over the bar. I wasn't sure if they noticed me, but I had made sure my stool was on the route to the restrooms. Sooner rather than later, I would be noticed.

Unfortunately, Susan spotted me on her way to the restroom. The worst possible result. If she brought me to the attention of the group, both our covers were blown.

I needn't have worried.

"What are you doing here?" she snarled, slurring her words just enough to let me know she'd been here awhile.

I cursed quietly. This was not the first time I'd seen her in this condition and the results of her work while inebriated were far from stellar.

"Just seeing if I can help."

"Help somewhere else." She turned away and headed for the ladies' room.

I wanted to be gone by the time she returned and frantically tried to get the bartender's attention. He took his time cashing me out, and in the interim, one of the FWC officers passed by my stool. I was hopeful he hadn't noticed me, but before entering the alcove to the restrooms, he turned back and looked directly at me.

"Hunter, isn't it? There's a group of us over there with your coworker, Susan. Come on over and join us."

He must not have gotten the memo that I had the plague. I was in deep now and needed to make a move before Susan returned. If she saw the two of us talking, it could get ugly, and if I joined the group in her absence it would be worse. Begging off, I finally got my credit card back from the bartender and, learning the lesson to pay cash up-front next time, headed for the exit. Sitting in the truck, I wondered what other kind of badly conceived trouble I could get in before Justine had any results.

Trying to pull out of my investigative death spiral, I called Ray. I'd never asked him about where he sold his product. I knew fishermen worked strange hours and, in order for the buyers to get the catch fresh from the boats, they had to ensure they were accessible to the fishermen. After today's scuffle, I would rather have talked in person, but he was a twenty-minute car ride, then a forty-minute boat ride, away.

Ray answered quickly. He kept his cool as I explained the threats that Scott had made against him, and promised to keep a low profile. I'd rather that he said he would stop selling, but it was his life. In return for promising to keep his identity out of my investigation, he gave me two names. Only one had an address; the second was a boat.

If there was one thing I had learned about locals, both here and in my previous job in rural California, is they believe they have a claim to the local resources. Be it dredging for gold in the streams of Northern California or selling seafood here, residents think being born in a place entitles them to extra privileges the rest of us are not granted. I sympathized with Ray, but didn't agree.

Sitting in my truck, I decided that it would be easier to check out the land-based enterprise first. The boat sounded like a better venue for a sketchy buy, but locating it would be more difficult, and it seemed like the logical thing to at least eliminate the real business. Hayward was selling legal tails, but he was in the same position as Ray: Neither had a commercial fishing license.

Back in my maps app, I typed the address in. The location was only a fifteen-minute drive, and I followed the directions to South Dixie Highway in Coral Gables.

The business was larger than I expected—too big to be buying from small-timers like Ray or Hayward. I was bothered that I now classified Ray and Hayward together. Pulling into the parking lot, I circled the premises, noticing the large walk-in freezers in back. After circumnavigating the entire property, I pulled up to the front door. From my truck I could see a "Closed" sign, but it offered an after-hours number. Security cameras were visible on the corners of the building and by the entry. Since there was no point in concealing myself if I already had been recorded, I got out, took a picture, and left.

The boat was my next stop, except without an address it wasn't easy. Ray said they hung out under the bridge over Bear Cut. It was an out-of-the-way location, but easily accessible from both land and water. Most boat traffic used Government Cut, just to the north, leaving the smaller crossing, with Key Biscayne the only land beyond, as a backwater.

Pulling back onto South Dixie Highway, I turned left and headed toward the Rickenbacker Causeway. Servicing several parks and beaches, the only commercial areas the roadway serviced were the Seaquarium on Virginia Key and the small community of Key Biscayne. This time of night, the road was quiet.

The first span over the main waterway was long and high, constructed with sailboats in mind. I cruised over it and reached the second bridge where I could see the lights from several boats below the structure. At first, I thought I had made a mistake in coming by land, and this operation might have been more productive if I had come by water. But since there was no boat traffic I would have been seen approaching from miles away.

Turning back to my trusty map app, I zoomed in on the area and found a small dock area labeled Darwin Beach. After a quick Google search, I discovered it was on the grounds of The University of Miami's Rosenstiel School of Marine and Atmospheric Science, and the pier was an extension of a bar called the Wetlab, run by the students there. Sounded like a perfect cover to observe the goings-on of the boats anchored under the bridge.

I drove through the small campus and parked near the bar. The only way to describe the place was "chill"—one of those places Justine and I would enjoy. Having learned my lesson earlier, I paid cash for a beer at the bar and took it outside, where I sat alone at a small table overlooking the water. I didn't have to wait long before a boat moved in. I grabbed my beer and headed toward the end of the pier for a better look.

19

STEVEN BECKER
A KURT HUNTER MYSTERY
BACKWATER FLATS

Sitting out by the water drinking beer and staring at the boats under the bridge might have been the most comfortable stake-out I'd ever participated in. The sound of voices from the boats wafted across the water, but even with the favorable breeze bringing them toward me, they were too faint to make out any words. I thought about moving to the beach to get closer, but figuring I would stand out like a cormorant against the white sand, I decided to order another beer and stay put.

The smaller boat appeared just to be looking for bait. With green lights shining into the water to attract the forage fish, the driver idled around the pilings. Another man was standing patiently on the bow with a cast-net loaded and ready to throw. With half the net over his shoulder and the other half draped by his side, he stood like a statue. The driver must have seen something and moved to the bow with a small bucket. He started tossing what I guessed was some kind of chum into the water. A long minute later, the man with the net whispered something and the driver stepped out of his way. Coiling his body, he swung the net out, snapping his wrist at the last minute so it would open fully. I'd seen Ray throw a net before and tried it once or twice, failing miserably with my attempts. The man showed his expertise, as the net opened and landed like a pancake. He waited for the lead weights attached to its perimeter to sink, then started to pull the line, which drew the bottom of the net shut and trapped the bait fish inside.

The driver moved forward again, ready to scoop the catch into the bait well. The scales of small silver fish reflected the moonlight as they were hauled aboard, and both men worked to free them from the net without injury. When the last fish was in the bait well, they started the procedure over again.

With the action on repeat there, I glanced over at the boat I should have been watching all along and saw that a smaller boat had pulled alongside. I had been so mesmerized by the men catching bait that I had missed its approach. I thought for a second about heading back to the truck and grabbing my binoculars, but was worried about being seen if their glass caught a reflection. Watching the water was a popular pastime and, within the confines of the bar's outdoor seating, nothing unusual. As I weighed the risk of getting the binoculars, I saw a figure climb from the smaller boat to the larger. Even if I'd wanted to, I had no time to retrieve them now.

Stuck where I was, I slid the chair a few feet closer to the rail and settled in to watch. I could see three men talking on the deck of the larger boat. Between the occasional road noise, the bait boat's idling engine, and the distance, it was impossible to make out what they were saying. Actions proved to be enough, as two men climbed back to the smaller vessel and grabbed a cooler that they heaved up to the deck of the larger boat. I could tell by the effort that it was heavy.

Even illuminated by the boat's spreader lights, and aided by binoculars I could not see the contents. Two heads peered inside, while the man from the smaller boat stood back with his arms crossed and a smile on his face. I guessed he was looking forward to a big payday, but the buyers appeared to have other ideas.

The cooler lid slammed shut and an argument ensued. I wasn't sure if it simply was a heated negotiation or heading to violence. The captain reached into his pocket. I feared a weapon, but he withdrew a rolled up stack of bills. After removing the rubber band the fisherman started counting. I followed along, stopping at twenty. If they were hundreds, the fisherman had done well for himself, if they were twenties, not so much, but I expected the former.

After unloading the cooler, the men shook hands, and the fisherman grabbed the handles of the cooler, easily setting it back on his boat before climbing down after it. There were some mumbled words, then the fisherman idled away. He cleared the bridge pilings, and I could hear the engine increase in pitch as the boat reached its cruising speed. Seconds later the white running light was a tiny dot on the horizon, and another minute after that the boat was enveloped by the dark night.

With their business concluded, the men who'd bought the contents of the cooler started to move around the boat. One went to the wheel, and the other to the bow, where he waited by the anchor line. I couldn't officially detain them from this distance, but I at least had to find out where they docked their boat. Standing by myself, a hundred yards away, on solid ground, I didn't have any way to follow—until the bait fishermen idled past.

Not wanting to alert the larger boat, I called out as quietly as I could to still allow my voice to reach them. It didn't, as the men only waved at me in response. The larger boat had idled over their anchor and the bait fishermen were moving past me.

I was out of time, and yelled at the bait boat, ordering them in my special-agent voice to stop. To reinforce my standing, I pulled my credentials from my pocket and flashed a badge.

My voice had carried to the larger boat, and both men turned toward me, but now the distance worked in my favor as they were too far to hear my words. Waving the bait boat over, I explained I was with the National Park Service and needed their help. They idled closer, probably thankful that I wasn't an FWC officer, which is what I hoped I looked like to the larger boat. My ruse appeared to work, as I could see the sense of urgency as the men tried to free the anchor. While the smaller bait boat approached the pier, the larger boat started to turn. A puff of grey smoke billowed the night's black backdrop as they started to move away.

The man at the wheel of the bait boat was clearly nervous and taking his time moving toward the dock. When he was several feet from the pier, without warning, I launched myself, crossing the three feet of water and landing on my feet in the bow. Glancing up at the bridge, just beyond I saw the buyer's boat's stern dig into the water as it fought to get on plane.

"I need to follow those guys," I told the man at the wheel.

"With this old rust bucket?" He pushed down on the throttle and the engine coughed. The other boat was through the bridge and made a turn to the north.

Water splashed out of the bait wells and the two fifty-five gallon drums they had tied to each side of the transom. Filled with water plus bait, they each weighed close to five hundred pounds. The boat would never get up on plane with that much weight in the stern. "Alright. I'll find another way. Drop me at the pier."

"Shoot, man, we know those guys," the man who had thrown the net said.

"Where do they keep the boat? I'm not looking to bust them, but they may have some information critical to a murder case I'm working on," I said, trying to coerce their cooperation.

"That officer, Hayward?"

"Yeah. You know him?"

"Nah, stayed away from that dude. We've got all our paperwork in order, though."

"Did he sell to those guys?"

"Seen him come up in a small bay-boat several times a week during season."

It took either a photographic memory—or an app—to keep track of the open and closed seasons for the myriad of Florida fish and shellfish species, but when someone said "season" in South Florida or the Keys, it usually meant lobster season.

He had dropped the boat to an idle, allowing us to talk over the old two-stroke engine, though he did have to goose the throttle a little to maintain steerage as the tide pulled us through the bridge.

"What do you know about those guys?" I asked

"Who'd you say you were with?" Cast-net guy asked.

"Special Agent Kurt Hunter, with the National Park Service. Hayward's murder occurred inside the park, making it my case."

"They teach you blind ninja stuff in secret-agent school?" Cast-net guy asked.

He was starting to grate on my nerves. Moving to the cooler, he pulled out another beer, his second in the few minutes I had been on board. Fortunately, the man at the wheel told him to get lost, and he moved back by the stern.

"Wish I could throw a net like him," I said.

"He's a one-trick pony. Sucks at everything else."

I wasn't going to argue that. Working the current, the driver had us close to the pier.

"You have fenders?" I asked.

He called to his partner, who put out two large, red balls and readied a line. "You want to find those guys, head up the river. Past the airport there's a sketchy marina with a bunch of fishing boats. Not what I call a premium spot, but they'll be there."

Nudging the throttle and using the red balls, he kept enough pressure against the dock that the line wasn't necessary. I thanked him and disembarked.

Walking through the Wetlab, I crossed the parking lot to my truck and sat inside, wondering if it was safe to check out the marina at night. I knew exactly where it was, and actually had been there several times working on another case. The three sides of the property bordering land were protected by an eight-foot-high chain-link fence with razor wire looped around the top. The easy access was by water.

Promising myself I was just taking a boat ride to check things out, I rationalized that using our personal boat was the best choice. Driving back over the Causeway and after merging onto 95, I took the second exit and cruised the surface streets to the small marina where Justine and I kept our center console. It, like everything in Miami, was protected by chain-link fence. Pulling up to the entrance, I entered my code into the keypad and waited as the gate slid open. I parked right by the boat and hopped aboard. A few minutes later, I was motoring upriver.

The almost six-mile-long Miami River bisects the city, running from the Miami Canal in the Everglades to Biscayne Bay. Its original headwaters are long gone, the small falls removed when the great "River of Grass" was drained to make room for development. As you move east to west you can see the property values drop. At the river's mouth are luxurious condos with million-dollar yachts docked nearby. The further inland you travel, as I was now, the lower the rent, until just west of the airport the banks of the river turned industrial.

I passed the police impound and evidence lot on the left and continued to the dicey marina that the bait fisherman told me to try. Security lights illuminated the seawall and pothole-scarred parking lot. Several larger boats were tied up along the seawall, with smaller ones, the size of the one I was looking for, docked in side canals that had been dredged perpendicular to the river. In the second one I found the boat I wanted.

Its spreader lights were on and the two men were unloading their "catch." Idling by, I waved, as boaters generally do, and continued upriver trying to figure out how to get, if nothing else, a picture of the boat. In addition to its registration numbers, there was a larger set stenciled on the side—its commercial fishing license.

The scam started to make sense. With a commercial license, they were allowed to sell as much seafood as the legal limits allowed. Where they got their catch from was anyone's guess—but I knew where they got their lobsters.

20

STEVEN BECKER
A KURT HUNTER MYSTERY
BACKWATER FLATS

ONCE PAST THE AIRPORT EXPRESSWAY, THE WATERWAY LOST whatever "river" feel it had. Looking ahead, it was dead straight and dredged, with small canals running off it. I wanted to make a turn and come back without looking suspicious. From a half-mile away, I could still clearly see the lights of the fishing boat at the dock. If they happened to look my way, they would see the red light marking my port disappear, then turn green as I came back toward them. There was a good chance they would ignore me as a lookie-loo if they happened to notice, since there was a fair amount of traffic on the river and canals, but it wasn't worth it. Continuing for another quarter-mile, I killed the navigation lights and went dark.

Hoping the shadow of my boat was invisible from this distance, I made a quick one-eighty and, after a couple hundred yards, turned the lights back on. I had my phone ready as I again approached the fishing boat, ready to take a picture. With my pen in my mouth, my notepad sat open on the helm ready to record the license and registration numbers, too. Redundant systems.

I was sitting about a quarter-mile away when I saw the lights of another boat approaching the dock. I shouldn't have been worried, but there was something familiar about its lines.

Turned out my gut was right.

With only a hundred yards separating us, there was enough ambient light to see the approaching boat was the twin-engine FWC RHIB. To make matters worse, there were two people standing at the helm—and one of them was a woman. Another fifty yards closer and I could see it was Robinson and Susan McLeash. Neither knew my personal boat, and since they were focusing on the fishing boat, I guessed they hadn't noticed me.

I had a decision to make. Remaining unseen was my priority, but I badly wanted to see what these two were up to. I'd noticed a side channel on my approach and, looking down at the chart-plotter, saw it was ahead, just past the dock. Moving into the shadows on the north side of the river, I put as much space between the FWC boat and mine as possible. Turning my head away as the boats passed one another, I couldn't see if they were looking at me. Assuming they hadn't identified me, I cut across the river and entered the canal.

Turning even a small boat like mine in the tight confines of the canal was like navigating a three-point turn with a car, only about a half-dozen more steps. Now facing towards the river, I crept up to the intersection and dropped to an idle. The original flow of the river had long ago been altered by the South Florida Water Management District. With what was left of the Everglades retained by a half-dozen locks upstream, and no tidal pull this far upriver, there was virtually no current here.

From my vantage point, I could see both boats. It appeared that Robinson, too, had scoped out the fishing boat on the way upriver, then turned and come back. The difference was, he had no interest in stealth. Bright LED blue and white lights suddenly shot out from the top of his T-tower as he made his presence known.

Robinson's voice echoed across the water as he called out to the fishermen to remain where they were and prepare to be boarded. In the confines of the canal, this was a whole lot of drama, but effective, as the men froze in place.

Leaving the emergency lights on, he approached the docked fishing boat, idling several feet away while Susan tossed fenders over the gunwales and worked the lines. It probably looked like a routine stop to the fishermen, but the truth was that Robinson and Susan were both outside their jurisdictions—though a haze of alcohol might have stretched those boundaries in their minds. If asked, Susan could justify being here. She was technically doing what I asked. Robinson, I wasn't so sure about.

It was a recipe for trouble, especially post-happy-hour. Feeling helpless, I sat there. All I could do was watch and wonder what was being said. The light bar was acting like a strobe, distorting the scene, everyone's movements jerky and in slow motion. It caused me to miss the gun coming out, and I was caught off-guard when I heard a shot fired.

I knew her history. That shot came from Susan.

Any law enforcement within hearing range would automatically respond to the gunshot and issue an alert to others in the area. With the lives of two agents in jeopardy, I had to abandon my cover and speed toward the boats. All four people were still standing—that was the good news.

The bad news was that the gun, as I had expected, was in Susan's hand.

"We've got this, Hunter," Susan slurred from across the two feet of water that now separated our boats.

With Susan distracted by my arrival, Robinson took the opportunity to disarm her. He didn't look at me or comment. Instead, he swung the gun barrel toward the two fishermen.

"We ain't done nothing wrong! Why'd that crazy bitch shoot?"

Robinson ignored the comment. I could see Susan's face, and as she started to respond, Robinson said something I couldn't hear and she backed down. But I knew our girl, and she wasn't done. Robinson stepped to the gunwale and, in what looked like a feeble attempt to justify the gunshot, took the fishermen's driver and fishing licenses, along with the boat papers. With the IDs and documents in hand, he moved back to the helm and, after laying the papers out on the leaning post, punched a number in his phone, and placed it to his ear.

I was sure my presence had changed Robinson's plan, though I wasn't at all sure why he was here. I guessed he was cleaning up Hayward's mess. Now the best he could hope was that one of these men was already wanted for something. A prior bench warrant would solve all his problems.

And then things got worse.

Susan, out of patience, slid in front of the console and, before Robinson realized what she was doing, started screaming at the fishermen. Robinson turned to me like it was my job to control her. I shrugged and continued to watch the show.

Susan had caught all the men off-guard, and I hoped one would slip and reveal something. Turned out the revelation came from her.

"Which one of you fuckers killed him? I know it was one of you!"

They backed away as she leaned forward. As far as I knew, these men had done nothing wrong other than maybe buying some seafood instead of catching it, which they could have done legally. They didn't deserve to be punished by Susan's rant before any charges were filed, and maybe not even then.

Robinson continued to peruse their paperwork, hoping for a break that would absolve him from any wrongdoing and justify his appearance here. On the bench seat were two piles of documents: ones that he had already verified over the phone, the others that he hadn't. The former was quite a bit higher and, from his expression, I could tell he knew he was running out of opportunity.

"I loved him! Why—"

Susan's exclamation turned my attention to her. She backed away and sat, head in hands, on the cooler in front of the console. Robinson appeared not to notice her, leaving me to clear this train wreck from the tracks.

Without asking, I tied my boat to the RHIB and crossed the gunwales.

I caught a sick expression on Robinson's face. It was his gun that Susan had fired. She'd pulled the same trick on me before, and I sympathized with the inquisition he was about to face. He would eventually be vilified and Susan would be suspended again. The result aside, the process was ugly.

"You okay?" I asked her. I sat on a small storage locker built into the hard bottom of the inflatable's deck.

"Kurt, we were getting along so well. I thought he might be the one." She sobbed.

I was not without compassion, but I'd seen this show before. Both acts: the wailing Susan McLeash, and the boyfriend who was "the one."

To their credit—and/or innocence—the fishermen had remained aboard their own boat. There had been ample time, with me dealing with Susan, and Robinson running the paperwork, that they could have snuck off. I knew the boatyard was enclosed with a chain-link fence topped with razor wire, but if they paid for a slip here, they likely had a key or code to open the gate.

Robinson had wasted no time in canceling the automatic calls for backup. The flashing lights on the street from the first responders, which had quickly appeared near the canal, had disappeared almost immediately.

"I'm going to talk to the fishermen. Wait here and I'll make sure you get home," I told Susan. Though she was drunk, I was careful not to mention that I would be her escort. She looked up, revealing the tracks of her tear-streaked mascara, and nodded. Robinson was still busy behind the helm, doing whatever he could to remain separate from the action.

"You okay if I come aboard?" I asked the fishermen, figuring a little civility after what had happened was in order.

"You got a warrant or anything?" The one who had been behind the wheel asked.

"No, just want to talk. I've got no interest in fishing or seafood."

"Just keep her under control." His eyes shifted to Susan.

I nodded and stepped on the gunwale of the park service soft-sided boat. Using the T-top's structure for support, I stepped onto the sturdy deck of the fishing boat.

"Kurt Hunter, special agent with the National Park Service." I extended my hand.

"We should file a complaint," the man by the stern whined.

The other man, likely the captain, turned to him. "Not right now. Why don't you go get a beer and start cleaning up? I expect this'll be over soon, right, Hunter?"

"Just a few questions and you can go."

"What about him?" The captain glanced at Robinson.

"You got no outstanding warrants, I don't think there's anything he can do," I replied.

"Okay, I'll answer your questions. Just keep an eye on her."

Susan had inadvertently insured a level of cooperation I wouldn't have gotten if she hadn't tried to shoot this guy. Good cop, bad cop taken to the extreme.

"How about we start with why she wanted to shoot you?" I watched his face carefully. After the previous events of the evening, there was little question he was on the wrong side of the law somehow, even if it was for as small an infraction as buying seafood—a product he was permitted to catch. Providing that his sales logs were legit, the acquisition end of his business was undocumented, relying on only hook and line, nets, and traps. Unless there was an eyewitness to his purchases, his under-the-table dealings would never be discovered. There had to be an accounting slight of hand to write off the expense for paying what he was expected to have caught, but that was none of my business

"Yeah, bought some stuff from Hayward. Mostly tails and all legal."

He probably had no idea, nor did he care, how Hayward had obtained the product.

"So, it was an equitable arrangement between you guys?" I was fishing to see if there was blackmail or extortion involved by Hayward.

"A little streaky. You couldn't count on steady production. But we had no issues."

"Any idea if he's involved?" I made a motion with my head toward Robinson.

"We all know who he is. First time I've seen his fat ass in a boat, though."

Reaching into my pocket, I removed a business card and handed it to him with the standard spiel, *if you think of anything, give me a call.* He took it and thumbed the corner, giving me the feeling he had something more to say.

"I got no dog in this fight," I said, trying to put him at ease.

"That one," he said, looking directly at Susan. "If I were you, I'd keep an eye on her."

For me this was old news but, coming from an outsider, the warning caught my attention. As I thanked him for the chat, I wondered just what Susan was up to.

21

Hopping back onto the FWC boat, I waited while Robinson handed the papers back over the gunwales and told the fishermen they were free to go. Knowing Robinson's passive-aggressive tendencies, he would probably say nothing negative about Susan's actions or my presence here tonight, but file a complaint about us with Martinez in the morning.

The two fishermen lifted a heavy cooler between them and set it on the dock. It appeared the fishermen felt they were vindicated. If they had something to hide they would have locked up the boat and bolted when Robinson handed back their paperwork. One of the men stayed with the cooler in case Robinson changed his mind, while the other walked into the darkness. A minute later a pair of headlights flashed and a battered pickup appeared, pulling up next to the dock. The men loaded the cooler in the bed and, without a look at us, headed off into the night.

The only question that remained was what to do with Susan. Robinson, as I had expected, was just standing behind the wheel as if waiting for me to deal with her. Despite her inebriated condition, in some twisted way our rocky history linked us together.

"Come on. I'll take you home." I reached down for her hand. There was no thank you, tearful or otherwise. She simply took my hand and followed me to my boat. It did occur to me that I would be taking her on my personal boat, but I doubted in her condition she would remember. Proving me correct, she turned, moved toward the bow and crumpled into a heap on the deck. I was fine with her passing out, but would have felt better if she had chosen the stern—downwind, just in case.

I'd left my phone on the shelf above the helm, and turned it over as I eased away from the FWC boat. Robinson stood stoically at its helm, waiting while we drifted away. I pushed off, creating a gap between the two boats. As soon as it opened up, he slammed the throttles and took off downriver. I was alone now, and checked my phone. Justine had left two messages, one a smiley face emoji, the other a more urgent, CALL ME! Checking the time, I saw the second message was left less than five minutes ago.

Crossing to the other, less populated bank of the river, I called her back.

"What's this about gunshots on the river?"

I figured it wouldn't take her long to find out there had been an incident. Any time her "coworkers" found out I was involved in something, they tossed daggers at my back by telling her. As my grandfather said, a little *schadenfreude*.

"Hey. All good." I tried to defuse the bomb before it went off.

"Couldn't just sit at home and wait, eh, kemosabe"

The nickname assured me she wasn't too angry.

"You know how it is." I idled forward, telling her the events of the past few hours as I traveled downriver.

"I get off in an hour," she said. "Got some results for you."

"I've got a small errand I have to run first." I explained about my passenger. Fortunately, she got it.

"Tuck her in and get back here asap. This is good stuff."

"Roger that. See ya soon." Taking a deep breath, I looked at Susan, curled up in a fetal position on the deck. We'd done this dance before. Tomorrow would be another day with no recognition of tonight's charity. Looking behind me, I checked my wake and goosed the throttle, trying to get a few more knots out of the engine without disturbing the boats docked alongside the river. The sooner this deed was complete, the better.

I reached our marina on the river, and after securing the boat, got the truck and pulled it alongside. Susan hadn't stirred at all on the ride. Grasping her arm, I slung it over my shoulder and lifted her from the deck. Somewhere along the way, she regained consciousness and slugged me in the stomach.

"Easy, girl, it's Kurt, just trying to get you home."

"Oh, Kurt!"

She sounded manic. I wasn't sure if she was laughing or crying and considered throwing her in the bed of the truck. Somehow, she sensed this and staggered to the passenger door, where I folded her in. then glanced at the seatbelt. Gritting my teeth, looking past her bulging blouse cut two sizes too small, I reached across her, trying to avoid contact, and successfully pulled out the seatbelt and secured it without touching her—possibly my major accomplishment of the day.

By the time we reached her condo, she was somewhat coherent and able to make it to the door herself. Watching from the truck, I waited until she was inside. My work here was done, and I hightailed it back home to our condo.

Two odors clung to me as I walked past Justine and headed for the shower: Fear and perfume. Fear has a distinct smell, and after the gunshot earlier, my pores had emitted it. Susan's overpowering perfume concealed the fear, but I admit it was still there.

After soaping up and rinsing twice, I stepped out of the shower, immediately feeling better.

"Hungry?" Justine called out from the kitchen.

I walked up behind her, glancing over her shoulder at the frittata browning in a cast-iron skillet, before I leaned in and kissed her neck. Elbowing me in the stomach, she pushed me back, pulled the pan from the stove-top, and slid it into the oven.

"You've got five minutes until this bad boy is done. Talk..." She sat down at the kitchen table.

I had other ideas, but there is no deterring a hungry woman.

When Susan McLeash and gunshots get mixed together, my senses seem to go on full alert, my subconscious working overtime to memorize things I might normally never remember. As I recapped the details of the incident to Justine, I pulled out my pad of paper and started making more notes, knowing by tomorrow I would likely forget something.

The timer on the stove dinged and interrupted me. Justine hopped up while I continued writing, and dished out two nice portions of her frittata. We fit well together in a lot of ways, and one of these was when eating. Always dining with someone who ate at a different speed—though this might sound nitpicky—could be extremely frustrating. Justine and I were silent eaters. The only conversation we had while we ate was to ask to pass the salt.

Our meal complete, I took the dishes to the sink and rinsed them off.

"Okay. Your turn," I said to her.

"Got a few hair and skin samples back from the gauges. Traces of blood, too."

"Evidence. Awesome." It sounded good, until she added a qualifier.

"It's all worthless with nothing to compare them to. You've handled enough lobsters. What you're calling evidence also could be considered normal. Those suckers can draw blood just by looking at them. I'd guess if you tested our gauges, you might get the same result."

My mind was racing through possibilities, searching for any hold to grasp. DNA and blood: It didn't get any better than that. "Hayward's and Scott's are on one, for sure. But what if there was a third person?" I waited for her to disqualify my statement. There could easily have been ten people who handled the gauges. I was clinging to a thin strand of hope that Hayward would have been very careful in keeping tabs on his doctored gauges.

"I can run what I have through a database, but you know the sample size is limited."

"Yeah, to felons and federal employees." As I said it, I wondered if the state required that the DNA of their employees be kept on file. Flipping the pen in my fingers, I almost put it in my mouth, but then stopped and handed it to her.

"What about this?" I asked, gesturing to the pen.

"What about it? You just buggered it all up."

"Robinson stuck the tip in his ear," I told her.

"That's gross!"

"But testing it is doable, right?" I asked her.

"Got blood for me, too?"

"If my hunch is right, you have it. It's Hayward's blood."

"You know, DNA tests take time, right?"

"Tomorrow will be fine," I said, and headed for the bedroom. The day had gone long and the adrenaline surge from earlier had worn off, leaving me drained.

I smiled and fell onto the bed, only to wake up in my clothes several hours later as the dawn's light barely filtered through the blinds. Justine was under the covers beside me, and I thought for a long minute about stripping down and joining her. But after the gunshot incident last night, I had a good idea I needed to do some damage control. Both Robinson and Susan would be spinning the story seven ways to hell.

Sliding out of bed, I grabbed a change of clothes from my drawer, and headed for the shower. At most I'd gotten three or four hours of sleep, and I was feeling it. I wolfed down a large chunk of the leftover frittata while the coffee brewed, and a few minutes later, I sat in my truck with a stainless mug holding my coffee.

The coffee gave me a jumpstart, and I quickly browsed through whatever I had missed on my phone. Still being the dark of night—or early morning, depending on your perspective—there were no new messages and only a few administrative emails. I set the phone on the seat next to me and quickly scanned my personal phone. With nothing there either, I took another sip of coffee and pulled out of the lot.

Traffic seems to run in fifteen-minute intervals here. There was often a huge difference in leaving at six forty-five versus seven. I was already past that window at seven-thirty and paying the price. Brake lights reflected off the slightly wet road in front of me, too wet to be just dew. I suspected a small storm had rolled through while I slept. To most, the light coating of rain made little difference to their lives, but to me it was an evidence-killer.

Justine would process Robinson's DNA from the pen, but I knew better than to expect the results back for close to a week. I wasn't sure I had that long. Usually, when Susan started firing weapons, you could assume a situation had reached a tipping point. This was the time when suspects made mistakes, and I turned onto the turnpike's southbound entry ramp hoping I would be there when it happened.

It didn't surprise me to see Susan's truck already in the lot and, from the wet asphalt below it, I knew it hadn't spent the night here. The woman recovered better than anyone I'd met, and I expected to find her in her office acting like nothing happened. With enough eye drops and pancake makeup, she would look like she did on every other day. It was eight-thirty already and Martinez's car was here as well. Hoping I hadn't missed any true confessions about the gunshot, or how she had spun the story so it was my fault, I hurried to the entrance and, after waving to Mariposa, took the stairs two at a time.

Even before I reached his office, I could see Susan's feet tapping nervously through the open door. Trying to be as nonchalant as possible, I approached, popped my head in, and said good morning.

"Is it Hunter?" Martinez waved me to the inside chair. "Is it?"

The space was tight enough that I had to brush against Susan to reach it. She glanced at me and looked back at our boss. I apparently had missed hearing her version of the story.

"So, can you explain why the only times we have incidents with our department personnel is when you are present?" Martinez asked me.

I wanted to answer that I was the only one doing any work, but that would only antagonize him. Instead I stayed silent, hoping he would reveal what Susan had told him.

"It appears that you've once again overstepped your bounds, Hunter."

22

When I was younger, I remembered tagging along to job sites with my dad. He had a way of diffusing customers with a simple line: "Whatever it is, it's my fault—just tell me what I did." That usually lightened the mood. Seeing the dour looks on Martinez and Susan's faces, I thought, *why not?* and let it rip.

"There's no laughing your way out of this, Hunter. Shots were fired with two of our agents in proximity, and not even in the park."

I took another risk, figuring he had to know Susan was lying or at least bending the truth. I just needed to provide an explanation that would exonerate her without embarrassing either of them. Maybe then we could get on with our investigation.

"The venue is unimportant. It is within our scope to pursue crimes committed inside the park outside of its borders." It was in the manual.

"Right," he said, pausing to figure out what to do with the way out I had just given him.

Susan seemed relieved as well.

"We were working independently pursuing a suspect," I added to reinforce the talking point to both of them. They quickly latched onto it and Martinez finally changed the subject to the investigation.

Depending on whether Robinson filed a complaint or not, the gunshot incident might be over. It had been Robinson's weapon that she fired. If I were a betting man, I'd wager that between Robinson's independent streak and his side business, we'd heard the last of the incident.

Too bad, because one of these days Susan might actually hit something.

Whatever Robinson did, Susan's ability to liaise with the FWC was compromised. Word would go out for his people to avoid her. Between Susan's new status as persona non grata, and Scott's firing, the lobster sanctuary idea was DOA. It had been a long shot anyway, though I had an idea to keep it alive. As much as the bureaucrats tried to bury ideas, those that cost little and made sense ended up eventually getting implemented despite them. Sometimes you have to be patient and wait. It was all good, except now I had to figure out what to do with Susan.

Martinez had returned his attention to his screens and, without any attention being thrown her way, Susan rose and left the office, allowing me a path to escape at the same time. I was on my way to the door when I heard my name.

"Sit, Hunter. And close the door."

Martinez wielded the intimacy of a private conversation like a sharp blade, and in this case, I had to assume I was going to get cut. I sat and waited.

"These interagency squabbles can be tricky and when investigations seem to drag on, things can get ugly."

Crossing, then uncrossing, my legs, I sat silently, hoping he would elaborate. The murder had occurred less than a week ago; I would hardly classify that as a "long time." I knew he was after information I didn't want to divulge at this point, but I was playing chicken with a master and finally caved.

"I've got some leads. DNA mostly, but the results won't be back for about a week."

"It's a start, but I'd like this wrapped up ASAP."

And I would like the murderer to present him or herself and confess. Neither of us was going to get what we wanted. I was burning through suspects: Scott was still there, but I could find nothing to pin him to the actual murder. I'd seen first-hand that he was hot-headed and impulsive, but was he so far gone he would kill his partner in the park service parking lot? It didn't make sense. I'd taken Scott off my radar for a day after his termination. Now I thought it might be a good idea to check in with him.

"I'd like to talk to Scott again, but I haven't seen his personnel file yet." There was no way Martinez was going to throw Susan under the bus, and I waited while he decided how to handle my request.

He placed his hands together under his chin in a subconscious prayer position. "I'll take care of it."

"I need his address, to start. That would help. Maybe checking out how things are in his private life, too. And a DNA sample couldn't hurt, either." Martinez's eyes flirted with his screens. He had lost interest. At this point I would be lucky to get an address. Visiting Scott at home might give me a chance to grab something for Justine to test. So far none of the evidence I'd brought her was admissible in court, but if she found anything that pointed me in the direction of the killer, I'd find something legit.

"Hayward's file, too."

"That I have." He swung around to face the trio of monitors on his side desk and moved quickly through several windows. "Here. I'll text it to you."

My phone pinged. After yesterday's close call, I had changed his ringtone back to the standard issue. I swear, he looked upset when he heard it and, avoiding eye contact, I glanced at the screen. His contribution to the investigation, however small it was, seemed to lift his mood, and when he continued to work the windows on his monitors, searching for some indiscretion that might have happened during our meeting, I rose and left, sure I heard him humming the Star Wars theme song on my way out.

Passing Susan's closed door, I figured it must have been nap time in McLeash land. How else could she survive?

Mariposa called me over just before I hit the door. Thinking it was something about Saturday, night I crossed the lobby to her desk.

"I got a hit on one of the inquiries I made."

I took a second to remember the bacteria and her calls to urgent-care facilities and hospitals. I'd asked only yesterday, but a lot had happened in the interim. She handed me a piece of paper with the information.

Pulling out my phone, I compared it to the address that Martinez had sent. I had a working knowledge of Coral Gables, an older Miami neighborhood known locally as just "The Gables." I thanked her and headed out to the truck feeling better than when I got there.

Hayward wasn't going anywhere, and I could get access to his house with a phone call. That made Scott's house my top priority, but when I entered all three addresses—Hayward's, Scott's, and the urgent care—into my map app to get a feel for their locations, the urgent-care center came up equidistant from the two men's residences, and surprisingly close to Susan's condo. Knowing who they had treated and for what could prove important, but with the myriad of HIPAA laws now in place, breaking down the barrier of patient privacy was an obstacle.

But after creating a plausible explanation for Susan being on the Miami River last night—and shooting at people, no less—

Martinez owed me one. I called and asked if he could help get the medical information. He promised he'd make some calls and see if he could get the patient file. I wanted the information before I saw Scott, and decided on a slight detour to kill some time. Hoping the Wetlab was open, I headed toward the Rickenbacker Causeway to see what the waterway under the bridge looked like in daylight.

The Wetlab was just about to open, and my uniform earned me early admittance. Promising I'd order lunch, I walked out to the pier from where I had seen the boats last night. Gazing out at the bridge, I wasn't sure what I was looking for, just hoping something would strike me. Around the water, things look different during the day, and this was no different. The first thing I noticed was how sketchy the approach was that the bait boat had taken to reach me last night. Had I known, without someone's life being in jeopardy, I never would have put them in that position.

The second thing I noticed was the construction of the bridge itself. The wide platform cantilevered over the supports below and was set close to the water with no high span for sailboats. Consequently, the water under the bridge was deep in shadows. A quick Google search showed the bridge had been restored about five years ago. In the process piers were added, making the support structure even more cluttered—ideal for a discreet rendezvous. There was no chance of being seen from the roadway above and little from the approaches. My current location was probably the best point to observe the goings-on.

Without a span for taller boats, Bear Cut got only a fraction of the boat traffic the main span of the Causeway received. Another plus for its varied uses. I had all but eliminated the buyers from my list of suspects, and the physical properties of the bridge only confirmed their dismissal. If I were in their position and wanted to kill someone, I would have chosen this venue over the parking lot at headquarters.

Scott and Robinson were now neck-and-neck for the top spot on my list. Ray's name was still on it, and Susan was all-too-close for comfort. Walking back to the restaurant, I took a seat at the bar with a view of the water and checked out the menu. While I waited for the bartender to take my order, I started playing with the jigsaw puzzle of suspects in my mind. I realized I had never confirmed either Scott's or Robinson's whereabouts at the time of the murder. Scott had just gotten off his shift and would have been close by, and Robinson had showed up far faster than I expected him, especially on a Sunday afternoon.

Susan had let me down, not even managing to get the personnel files from Robinson. I wondered how hard she tried. It was probably fifty-fifty whether it was because Robinson resisted or because she didn't ask.

Detective work can be described as ninety-nine percent drudgery and one percent uncontrollable craziness. I'd gotten a little taste of the one percent last night. Today was looking to be routine, or so I thought. Staring at the water, wishing I was on it, I saw a boat approach. It was up on plane, on a collision course with the bridge. The boat was close enough to the piers and running flat out. I was out of my seat, with my phone in hand, ready to help and call 911, when the hull suddenly dropped in the water, rising and falling as the wake ran underneath it.

At first the waves obscured the hull. Finally, they subsided enough for me to see it was the twin-engine RHIB, and there were two men aboard. The last few days were the most I'd seen the boat used in a year, leading me to believe that Robinson was somehow involved in all this. Running the department all these years without doing any work told me he was smart and shrewd. He had to be in on the scheme to confiscate and sell the lobsters. Martinez was a master at manipulating reports and numbers to get the outcome he wanted; I had to assume Robinson, or any other long-tenured bureaucrat, would be just as adept. With the majority of the tickets being issued for safety violations and few or none being written for short or out-of-season fish, he had to be involved. That didn't mean he killed Hayward, though. Scott had shown a mean streak, had access to the murder weapon, and the opportunity to kill Hayward. Whether his holier-than-thou attitude was enough for motive was the questionable part.

The boat's inertia continued to move it forward, bringing it awfully close to a piling. The driver cut the wheel to port in order to avoid striking the bridge pier. Though the rigid, inflatable hull would likely have withstood the impact, it was low tide now, and the two feet of exposed crustaceans could have easily penetrated the material. Both men's backs were to me as the guy at the helm accelerated to avoid the collision. Now I could see that Robinson was driving, and when the boat turned again, I was surprised to see the passenger, sitting on the bench, was Scott. Something was wrong with his posture. He seemed stiff, and after a second, I realized he was tied to the seat.

Scenarios flooded my mind—none good. Before I could react, another boat approached, this time from the mainland side. I knew it from a quarter mile away—the fishermen from last night.

23

STEVEN BECKER
A KURT HUNTER MYSTERY
BACKWATER FLATS

I wondered why they were meeting here. The boats were deep in the shadows, but the backwater flats of the bay might have been a better place to do whatever they intended to do. As I knew first-hand, bodies that were dumped or had drifted into those narrow, mangrove-covered channels were often unidentifiable after a few weeks. The same back-country predators that would assault a body were present here as well, predominantly crabs, and in addition, bull sharks were known to prowl these waters. Robinson might have thought the bay was too risky a meeting place. He knew I patrolled there, and he had turned most of the fishing guides against him. Here, he would have no reason to think I was sitting a hundred yards away watching them.

I had an idea what was coming and as the men talked, I tried to stay calm and judge the distance, current, and my ability to cross the span of water. Currents at the bridges during some tidal phases were in excess of four knots; faster than most men can swim. There would be no point in diving in to rescue Scott, fail at the attempt, and need to be saved myself.

Several brightly colored Styrofoam balls, markers for the

blue-crab traps below, were set in the deeper water beyond the rocks. Walking to the rail, I checked the flow of water around the buoys. Once the line was taut, a strong current would show a wake in the direction it flowed. It was pretty calm and only wind waves danced around the buoys, a good sign, but under the surface could be a different story. Moving my attention back to the boats, I saw something being lashed to Scott, likely a weight of some kind. It certainly appeared he was about to be dumped wearing the proverbial concrete shoes. I ran back inside, yelling at the bartender to call 911. Scanning the bar top, my eyes saw a knife he had been cutting fruit with. I reached over the bar top, grabbed it, and ran back outside.

Not expecting any action when I walked in the Wetlab, I had left my sidearm and duty belt locked in the truck. Tossing my phone, keys, and wallet with my credentials to the deck by a post, I stripped off my shirt and, tossing it over my stuff, climbed over the rail. The rocks were slime-covered and fairly steep, forcing me to my hands and knees. I reached the water without incident and looked back across to the two boats sitting under the bridge.

Scott had been transferred to the fishing boat. Once his feet had cleared the gunwales of the RHIB, Robinson spun the wheel and idled to the next pier, where he gunned the twin engines and started back south. Whatever was going to happen next, his hands were clean. I waited, slinking across the rocks to get a better look. From this distance, even if I was seen I didn't think the fishermen could identify me. I hoped to look like a tourist trying to catch crabs. Once I was in the water, it would be a different story. My best course of action for this instant was inaction.

The wake from Robinson's boat had dissipated, leaving only the fishing boat under the bridge. The sun was overhead, leaving the underside of the structure deep in shadows. In the dim light,

I thought I saw one of the men strike Scott across the face. His head slumped forward and whatever resistance he had put up came to an end as each man grabbed Scott under an arm and hauled him to his feet. They nodded at each other and rolled the bound man over the gunwale. A crab trap followed, but no buoy floated to the surface. The concrete poured into the trap to hold it to the bottom would be enough to keep Scott below until the crabs and sharks finished him off. A few seconds later, ripples were all that were left of the location as the boat pulled away.

The second I hit the water I knew I had misjudged the current. The incoming tide had the water moving opposite the wind, counteracting the visible effect on the buoy. It felt like I was going nowhere as I stroked toward the bridge. Moving toward the rocks to get out of the main flow helped and I started making some progress. Working my way along the shore, I reached the pier closest to land in what felt like an hour, but I guessed was less than a minute. Crossing to the center would be more difficult, but fortunately a kayak appeared.

Waving my hands over my head in the universal signal for distress got the paddler's attention, but didn't alter his course. If I didn't get his help in the next few seconds, Scott would die.

"Police officer. I need your assistance!" I screamed, taking water into my mouth before the words were fully out. He must have heard something and I saw the bow turn toward me.

"Dude. You need some help?"

"Hurry." I didn't want to delay the rescue with an explanation. Paddling toward me as we talked, he was now close enough to reach me in a few strokes.

"Dude. What are you doing out here?"

"Guy's in the water over there." I counted the piers and pointed. "I'll grab on, just get me over there."

Dreadlocked and probably stoned, he was the only option

available. As it turned out he was an experienced paddler, and even then, it took all his ability to work the current and position the kayak where I wanted without smashing the boat or myself into one of the piers. I started breathing up, pulling huge breaths all the way into my diaphragm and letting them out my mouth, preparing to dive. I hoped since the bridge wasn't built for larger boats to pass under the water wouldn't be too deep where Scott's body was dumped.

Everything was moving in slow motion. Blood pounded in my ears as the clock in my head started ticking louder and louder. At what I estimated was somewhere into minute three, I figured we were on top of the site and released my grip on the kayak. With the depth unknown, I conserved my breath and rotated into a pike position, penetrating the surface as cleanly and effortlessly as possible.

The current decreased as I dropped what I guessed to be a dozen feet to the bottom, but now the visibility was my immediate concern. Able to see only three feet in front of me, I stood on the ground and spun in a slow circle. Seeing nothing, I expanded the search area.

The first contraction took me by surprise. I was far from an elite freediver, but had thought myself competent. I wasn't in the water a full minute before I was forced to surface. There was no time to breathe up. It had to be four minutes since Scott had been thrown over. Diving down again, this time not worried about my form, I frantically swam around the area.

The bottom was littered with debris. A good deal looked like old piers from the bridge's renovation. All the straight lines did make it easier to discern something that wasn't. Plenty of fish cruised the area and I thought I saw the shadow of something large in the darkness. I was just about to surface when I noticed movement near the bottom. Whatever it was appeared jerky and restrained, whereas fish were fluid and graceful. It had to be Scott.

I could feel my heart rate accelerate and knew I was past the point of rational decision-making. If I'd been able to reason, I would have immediately surfaced, breathed up, and descended with a line that I could tie onto Scott. Instead, I pulled through the water until I reached him and tried to do it myself. Scott was in full panic mode, making rescue even more difficult. Running on fumes, I had nowhere near the air or energy to haul him to the surface.

Using the fruit knife from the Wetlab, I cut the trap-line and I pulled as hard as I could, but Scott's dead weight was too much for me. Without being able to bring him to the surface alone, I sprung from the bottom. Gulping for air, I called for a line. My opinion of the dreadlocked stoner immediately improved when he reached back and pulled a tow rope from one of the compartments in his kayak. Holding the free end of the line, he tossed the bag to me. Taking a huge gulp of air, I grabbed the bag and descended, careful not to hinder the line as it released.

Scott was on his side and, unsure if I could lift him and snake the line under him, I pulled the remainder of the rope from the bag and tied the bitter end to the restraints around his wrists.

Before ascending I gave three hard tugs on the line, hoping the man above would start taking in slack while I made my way to the surface. Finally, my head broke through and I grasped for air.

"Dude, climb on and help. Got a big one here."

Still sucking huge gulps of air into my lungs, I slid onto the kayak. The kayaker had already taken the slack out of the line, but needed help to raise the body. Trying not to think of Scott as dead weight, I slid onto the kayak and kneeled next to the paddler. Again he surprised me as his wiry muscles contracted.

We pulled the line together. At first only the kayak moved, but when the line came vertical, with our combined effort we felt Scott's body rise through the water column. When directly underneath us, his weight started to pull the kayak under, forcing us to shift to the far gunwale. Finally, Scott's head broke through the surface.

"Dude, don't look like he's alive."

Ignoring him, I pulled Scott's upper body onto the bow. Fortunately, it was a sit-on-top model with a wide deck and supposedly unsinkable. I had to differ with the last description, when with our combined weight water started pouring onto the deck. Sliding off, I directed the kayaker to bring Scott to the pier.

Following in the kayak's wake, I rode the current back to the pier and started climbing the rocks. Hearing a siren's wail, I looked toward the bar. Hopefully the first responders had arrived. The kayak bumped against my leg, and I turned back to Scott. Grabbing the handle built into the nose of the kayak, I hauled it onto a rock, ignoring the stoner's complaints about scratching it. Once it was partially out of the water, I grabbed Scott in a fireman's carry and hauled him onto land.

Just as I reached the level surface of the pier, a group of uniformed men and women appeared. Waving them over, I stepped back to let the professionals work, and, breathless, collapsed onto the ground. One of the paramedics started to administer CPR while another placed an Ambu bag over Scott's mouth and nose. Hoping I had been in time, there was nothing I could do but sit back and watch.

"Dude, mind if I scram out of here? All these uniforms give me the willies." The kayaker scanned the growing crowd of paramedics, police, and firemen.

"No worries." He was an innocent passerby who ended up helping. I didn't see any need to include him any further. "Appreciate your help." I rose and shook his hand. He was clearly awkward with the traditional handshake, but I wasn't getting into the man-hug thing with him. Turning, he walked back to the pier, climbed over the railing into his kayak, and started paddling into the bay. With the current in his favor, he was soon just a dot on the water.

Turning my attention back to Scott, I watched the group around him working like a well-oiled machine. There was nothing I could do. Scott was unresponsive. I figured it was about ten minutes since he had gone in the water, but the responders' pace never slowed. Suddenly, the medic by his head jumped back to avoid the spew of seawater coming from Scott's mouth. Several minutes later, a wave of relief fell over me as I watched him sit up and start to breathe on his own.

I had to admit a little satisfaction. For once I'd pulled a live body from the water instead of a dead one.

24

The rescue vehicles blocking the entrance to the Wetlab had delayed the lunch hour. The action was over and the first responders were packing up to leave, although many still lingered. Not wanting some Miami-Dade patrol officer in the middle of my case, I figured I should stick around to the end. With no background details, the officers who were on-site were treating it as a straight-up rescue. I was the only witness to the actual crime and I intended to keep it that way—at least until Grace Herrera walked in.

For a man, the cheap business suits worn by male detectives were easy "fashion"—maybe not comfortable—but easy. For a woman, an ill-fitting, cheap suit was much harder to pull off. Columbo fostered the stereotypical image of a rumpled, wrinkled detective, and on men it worked. Some female detectives abided by this code, too.

Grace didn't. Her high heels clicked on the concrete floor as she approached. As I watched her coming toward me, "glamorous" was the word that came to mind.

Pulling off her larger-than-life sunglasses, she stared me

down. It was an intense look honed through years of being a good-looking woman in a man's world.

"Hunter. It seems you're always around when something out-of-the-ordinary happens."

"At your service." She was the kind of woman you wanted to flirt with. Making her smile felt good.

Our heads turned as the stretcher with Scott's protesting body strapped to it passed by.

He saw me and said, "I'm fine. I don't need this. Hunter, tell them to let me go home."

"You really should get a full evaluation. Maybe a CT scan or something." Scott spending some quality time in the hospital might be a good thing. He'd likely be safe there without me having to call in favors and assign a duty to watch him. Attempted murder of any law enforcement officer, whether they were well-liked or not, always rallied the troops.

"Can I at least make a phone call?" he asked.

I gave Grace the "got a minute?" look and she nodded. Walking over to Scott, I handed him my phone. He stopped complaining for a second, but my real motive was to see who he called.

Before he made his call he turned back to me. "Water?"

I was starting to feel like his man Friday, but realized something. I might miss his call, but my phone would record the number he dialed. After getting the bartender's attention and asking for a glass of water, he dumped some ice in the glass, filled it from the bar gun, and handed it to me. Before I walked away, I noticed a black plastic caddy with napkins and straws. Grabbing two straws, I stuck them in the drink and walked back outside.

"Here you go." I handed Scott the glass, hoping he would use the straws. I hadn't done a study on men and straw usage, but even before straws had become the latest environmental travesty, I never used one. Scott's position on the gurney forced him to, and after finishing the water, I took the glass back, making sure to slide the straws into my pocket. Justine would scold me about their care, but I had his DNA.

Back at the gurney, Scott finished his call and handed the phone back.

"Jackson Memorial?" I asked the paramedic.

He nodded and pushed the gurney toward the waiting ambulance.

"I saw that," Grace said. "Slick move. Want to fill me in?"

With the ambulance gone and the restaurant open, things started to return to normal—including my appetite. "Got time for lunch?"

She looked around. "Yeah, I'm already screwed standing here talking to you. Might as well get a meal out of it."

I was surprised it had taken so long, but as the last of the first responders were packing up, the media moved in. Three vans, each representing a different network, pulled up in quick succession. The last fire truck must have spotted them before me and hightailed it out of the parking lot.

The media's playing field had changed with the proliferation of smartphones. Once upon a time, in the not-so-distant past, there were liaisons from each department responsible for dealing with the media. Back then things were more professional. Video was edited and polished before airing in its allocated time slot on the news. Now, it was a race between those same liaisons posting on their department's social media channels, the raw, unedited footage that people wanted. In addition to that any bystander with a phone could have their video go viral.

Fortunately, the restaurant had been closed at the time of the incident and there were no witnesses aside from the staff. I could only hope, for the kayaker's sake as well as mine, that none had taken video. I glanced down at my phone, thinking that just in case, I should alert Martinez to monitor the social media platforms.

I was far from being a celebrity, but I'd been on several high-profile cases since landing here. Grace had her share as well. Standing together we were all too recognizable. I thought about canceling lunch, splitting up, and running.

Grace took a different approach. Plastering a photogenic smile on her face, she walked right into the bullets. Running was still on my mind, but one of the reporters noticed me and started walking my way. Taking the coward's approach, I followed Grace, using her body as a shield to deflect the onslaught of questions they were preparing to throw my way.

"Agent Hunter. There is a video of you saving the man under the bridge. Did you know it's going viral?"

I was done. One of the staff must have posted a video. As the cameraman moved around Grace, I glanced down at myself. The use of towels in South Florida is overrated. A few minutes in the sun is all that it takes to dry off. I'd put my shirt back on earlier, and quickly tucked it in and checked the buttons. A quick sweep of my hair and I left Grace's cover and took on the media.

"The Special Agent in Charge will give a statement later today," I told the scrum. Martinez lived for the podium. He would be happy to take credit for the rescue.

"Is this related to the murder of Officer Hayward?"

"Later today." I did my best Bill Belichick impression.

"Captain Herrera, do you have anything for us?" Another reporter called out.

She smiled again. "This investigation is under the National Park Service. We were just here to assist."

"Agent Hunter. The 911 call from the bartender said you were late getting in the water. Did you know this was going to happen, and did your delayed reaction endanger Officer Scott?"

I knew she was baiting me, and like a hungry marlin after a tuna, I took it. "This is an ongoing investigation." I stopped and tried to hold back, but she was in my personal space now, thrusting the phone toward my mouth.

"You're always looking for an angle, aren't you? What makes you think I did anything but be in the right place at the right time?" I stepped back. She followed.

"I'm just doing my job, Agent Hunter. Mine is reporting the news, not causing it."

I knew they'd edit her response. There was nothing I could do to take the words back. "Just following leads."

She pressed forward. "Care to elaborate?"

"Not at this time." Moving quickly now, I sought the protection of the restaurant. The reporter finally backed down and, as I felt the chill of the air conditioning hit me, I looked back and saw her deep in conversation with her producer, probably trying to figure out how to manipulate what I had said for maximum effect. Grace was right behind me and we followed the hostess to a table overlooking the bridge.

"Relax, Kurt, it's just us."

"Yeah, and the half-million people that watch that broadcast. I'm not very good at this."

"Focus on the positive. You saved a man."

"Investigation endangers a man's life is what I'm seeing for headlines." I couldn't get the reporter's question out of my head.

"Maybe you ought to call your boss and fill him in. I know how much he likes his face time."

"You're right." The waitress had approached, and I pointed to the burger I wanted on the menu, then stepped outside. I didn't mind if Grace heard the conversation, but I was leery of the other tables overhearing me. I passed the bartender on the way out, and gave him the evil eye for posting the video. He continued with whatever he was doing, oblivious of the curse I had put on him and his ancestors.

Standing by the railing, in the same place I had watched Scott being dumped into the water, I called Martinez.

"A phone call from Agent Hunter. This must be important." The sarcasm in his voice bit me.

"There's been some action and the media's involved now. I offered you up for a press conference this afternoon and didn't want you to get blindsided." He was silent, probably frantically scribbling notes as I recounted the morning's adventures.

"Never a dull moment with you, is there?"

"I might come off as sounding a little harsh on the video."

"Really." The sarcasm was back in his voice.

"They baited me."

"No worries, Hunter. I'll schedule it for four o'clock. Please give me an update before then."

No "attaboys" from the boss for saving a life. He was in total podium mode. I took a minute before heading back inside the restaurant and opened my DVR app, where I scheduled it to record the news. I couldn't wait to see how Martinez twisted this around to make it look like he had saved Scott.

The call had taken longer than I thought and when I sat back down, before I could start recounting the events of the last few days to Grace, our food arrived. I tried to slow down and chew, but found myself famished and inhaled the burger. Grace picked at her salad, waiting patiently. Pushing the empty plate aside, I started with the discovery of Hayward's body. I gave her the unabridged version. Grace was an ally, one of the few I had with Miami-Dade. Even if she was not involved with the case, I wanted to be sure she knew everything.

"What's your next step?" she asked. The interview phase was over.

I knew it was a casual question. I'd had a plan until Scott got tossed into the water. Now, things had changed. "Can we put a BOLO out for the fishermen?"

"For sure. What about Robinson?"

"I think some good old-fashioned detective work is in order."

She knew exactly what I was talking about. "Don't get caught, Kurt. Tailing another officer'll get you in a world of hurt if he finds out."

"We find the fishermen, it's a slam-dunk to hold them for attempted murder. I saw the whole thing."

"Any other witnesses?"

"We can check with the bartender. He saw enough to video the rescue."

"YouTube and Facebook are not making things easier on us, are they?"

I shook my head, wondering if Allie had seen the video yet. I'd call her as soon as Grace and I were finished. She'd get butt-hurt if she saw it without hearing from me. If a friend of hers saw it first, it would be even worse.

"Here." Grace slid her notepad across the table. "Give me whatever information you've got on them, and I'll send it out."

I wrote down a description of the men, their boat, and the marina where they docked. The server came by and removed our plates, dropping the check on a small clipboard before she left.

"I got this,"I said.

"Yes, you do. There's a fine line being seen around you, Hunter. It's all good if you find the perp, but if you don't there'll be hell to pay with the other detectives."

"Don't I know it. Thanks, Grace." I dropped my credit card on the table and sat back, trying to figure out how to deal with

Robinson. The attempted murder dropped Scott down a few notches on my suspect list, leaving Robinson in first place. The only problem was, after handing Scott over to the fishermen, it still didn't seem like Robinson had the stomach to murder someone in cold blood.

25

STEVEN BECKER
A KURT HUNTER MYSTERY
BACKWATER FLATS

GRACE AND I LEFT THE RESTAURANT, SAID GOODBYE, AND WALKED to our separate vehicles. The food filled the void left by the waning adrenaline and I was feeling a little better as I pulled out of the lot. With Scott's attempted murder occurring in Miami-Dade's jurisdiction, however they chose to prosecute, it would be their arrest. I only hoped Grace would get the credit for what looked to be a slam-dunk. I did hope to get an interview with the suspects once they were in custody, but until then, there was nothing I could do on this end.

Robinson had headed south from the bridge, probably back to the marina to ditch the boat. With nothing further to be gained by staying in Miami, I started back to headquarters hoping Martinez's surveillance network might prove useful in locating him.

Fridays saw an influx of tourists heading to the Keys for the weekend, and today was no different. With RVs and trucks towing boats, the usually light, midday traffic was stop and go. The never-ending construction on the southbound lanes of the turnpike didn't help either, but it wasn't as bad as it had been over the last year. Nearing completion, or at least no longer interrupting the flow of traffic, huge sound barriers were being erected to protect the neighborhoods adjacent to the highway from traffic noise. I used the time to leave a message for Allie, telling her to check out the news and asking about the weekend plan for her and her friend. She should have been in class, and even if she wasn't, she was smart enough not to answer the call. As I headed south, I worried about her driving down with her friend. She was pretty careful by herself, but in Miami traffic even the smallest distraction could prove deadly.

An hour later, I reached headquarters. It was about one o'clock, and with three hours until Martinez's press conference, I was anxious for news if the fishermen had been apprehended, I glanced at my phone. My screen showed no new notifications, but I still held out hope. Arrests being made would make Martinez's job considerably easier. It had already been a long day and I fought the urge to walk on by the park headquarters, hop on my boat, and head out on the bay. Martinez's surveillance forced my decision. Generally knowing my location with a three-foot accuracy, he texted that he was in his office.

Mariposa's smile helped. She gave some encouraging words about the rescue and I headed upstairs, where I expected the accolades would be considerably less. Susan's door was closed. I wasn't sure if she had been suspended again, or if Martinez had told her to leave early and disappear for the weekend until things quieted down. A savvy reporter would put the call about last night's gunshot together with Scott's rescue and the BOLO for the fishermen, and throw a hardball at Martinez. Susan being at work wouldn't help that cause.

Martinez barely looked up when I entered. Deep into his study of a handwritten speech, he glanced occasionally at the surveillance screens, then back to the paper. At first, I thought he didn't see me, but just before I was about to speak, he waved me to a chair.

"Interesting. Just give me a few minutes."

I tried to stop fidgeting while I waited, wondering what he wanted from me. I doubted it was to rehearse his speech.

It turned out he had found a real clue—not an FBI clue—something actionable. He turned the legal pad upside down, and hit a few keys. The screens changed, and I recognized the parking lot outside. Craning my neck to see, he broke down and invited me behind his desk for a better view.

Getting a serious "don't touch me" vibe, I got up and stepped behind his chair, trying not to invade his personal space. Leaning slightly over his shoulder for a better look, I almost set my hand on the back of his chair, but sensing him tense, I backed away. "When was this?"

"Afternoon of the murder." Simultaneously, he worked the keyboard and mouse trying to get the frame he wanted. "There." He stopped the playback and zoomed in on a figure in the parking lot.

Pressing the pause button, he advanced the image one frame at a time. A figure moved in and out of the camera's field of view with its back to the camera. It was only in a handful of frames and probably appeared as a blur in real time. It only took a glance to recognize Robinson.

"That's the camera mounted on the roof looking west?"

Martinez looked at me like I had broken his top-secret code. "Yes." He paused. "Camera locations are chosen as a deterrent, as well as for actual surveillance," he said, with a smug look.

I knew he was trying to justify his existence, but let it pass. The date and time were visible on the top right of the screen. Sunday at 15:43. "Timing works. I wondered how he reached the scene so quickly, especially on a weekend afternoon."

"I can't get a shot with his truck, either. Interesting."

"It's very circumstantial, but yes, it is a pretty big coincidence. Can you back up the video a few minutes before and let it play?"

"Sure." With a half-dozen keystrokes, the scene reversed.

"Any controls on the camera itself?" I had noticed it pan back and forth to cover the entire parking lot. "What if he was driving his personal vehicle?"

He looked across at me like I was an idiot. Government employees rarely used their own cars or trucks—especially the supervisors, whose work vehicles were generally newer. The camera passed by a park service truck and then another.

"Wait." I wished I hadn't said it the second the word was out of my mouth. Martinez didn't seem to notice, though. Monday through Friday, both trucks were generally there, but this was Sunday. I had a split-second to decide if I should tell him. He stared at me, waiting for me to elaborate.

"Nothing." I tried to rationalize my deceit. There was no way to tell what lengths he would go to protect Susan.

He continued to play the footage right through the time of the murder. A few minutes after Robinson appeared, Hayward could be seen walking to his truck. The camera moved away for the next few minutes. When it returned, Hayward's body was prone on the ground with a small pool of blood spreading from his stomach. The camera moved away again. When it returned, the blood pool was much larger. The time lapse showed the aggressiveness of the assault.

I asked Martinez to return to the frames of Hayward walking across the lot. Checking the timestamp as he scrolled though in slow motion, I waited until it made the second pass, showing his dead body. Three minutes had elapsed. Rounding things off, I figured the killer had a two-minute window to execute the murder.

"That takes things to a totally different level of premeditation," Martinez said, checking my math. "This wasn't a spur of the moment decision."

And that kind of reasoning is what got you promoted to Special Agent in Charge, I thought. I watched him to see if he could follow the yellow-brick road.

"The killer knew about the cameras," Kurt said.

I didn't bother to tell him that someone else could have passed on the locations. Especially as it appeared Susan McLeash had been there as well. Now, I had to find out if she was actually an accomplice, or an unwitting dupe; there was little chance she had been working on a Sunday. Robinson had abducted Scott, making him at least an accessory to the foiled murder attempt. I was wondering if he had any actual blood on his hands from Hayward's murder when my phone rang. Ignoring Martinez's questioning look, I glanced down at the display and saw it was Allie.

"Excuse me." I rose and left the office without giving Martinez a chance to comment. Hitting *Accept* I walked down the hallway, further away from his prying ears. Though there was always the chance of a listening device wired to his desk, I took the call.

"Hey,"

"Hey, Dad. Lana and I are going to head down there now."

Any father knows their daughters can confuse them in one sentence. "I thought your car was in the shop and your mom was going to drive you down?"

"Lana has a car. She's gonna drive. We'll be leaving here in about ten minutes. Just wanted to give you a heads-up."

I racked my brain trying to recall any information on Lana; bits and pieces of conversations filtered through my head, but I couldn't come up with anything solid. Allie living with her mom took me out of the day-to-day loop of her life. I had agreed to the arrangement, knowing it was better for the kids of split families to have a permanent residence. Juggling their lives one week to the next, moving between their parental unit's domiciles, disrupted their stability. Someone had to rise above and give in. In our case, at least initially, I hadn't had much of a choice. After the cartel firebombed our house back in California, Jane had wasted no time in dragging me in front of a judge. At the time I had to agree with my ex and her lawyer. I had no defense and waived my right to an attorney. Thinking I had accepted the consequences of my actions like a man, it had taken me a year to realize I had made a mistake, and then five figures given to my attorney, Daniel J. Viscount to correct it. I was hurt, but Allie was the one who was damaged. In her eyes, I had abandoned her. A lot of water had passed under the bridge since then, and Jane and I now had what I thought was an equitable custody arrangement. I had to credit Justine for her help in that.

"What kind of car? How long has she had her license? Has she ever driven in Miami traffic?" The questions kept coming.

"Dad."

It was becoming apparent I had little say in the matter. There are several milestones when raising a child. At first walking is scary, then school, but nothing is like driving. Their ability to suddenly be miles away from you in a matter of minutes without any control or oversight is daunting. Allie was a good kid, but I had no idea about Lana. Falling back on my last leg, I asked the one question that I tried to avoid: "Is it okay with your mom?"

"Yes. Lana's been taking me to school lately."

"Be careful." Defeated, I looked down at the floor, thinking maybe I should intervene in the repair of her car. If it only had a carburetor I could handle it, but the electronics were better left to a pro.

"See ya soon." She disconnected.

I hadn't really wanted to talk to her mom, but I would have exchanged the stress of the encounter for the knowledge that

Allie was at least safe. I knew I had to get over it. College was on the horizon and I knew things were only going to get worse. Allie was interested, and had the grades for, the University of Florida. Gainesville, though centrally located, was still a seven-hour drive from the park.

The hallway was quiet, with Susan gone and Martinez prepping for his press conference. I wandered down to my hole-in-the-wall and opened the door. Turning on the light, the only source of illumination in the windowless room, I sat at the desk and started processing the video I had just seen. I felt I needed to keep the discovery of Susan's truck in the parking lot at the time of the murder from Martinez. It wasn't to protect her, but more to buy me some time to figure out how to approach him without worrying about him getting defensive.

Once again, I'd covered for Susan last night. By giving witness to the perceived threat of the fishermen, I gave a plausible explanation for the discharge of Robinson's weapon. If that wasn't enough, I had driven her home. But faced with the choice of which of them to protect, if the two-headed monster of Robinson and McLeash were on opposite sides of a coin, I would call her name every time.

Checking the time, I figured I had two hours until Allie and friend arrived, and sent off a quick text to Justine as I headed out of the building. Martinez's door was closed. He was either putting the final touches on his makeup or had already left for the TV studio. Waving goodbye to Mariposa, she called me over.

"Did you have a chance to run down those leads?" she asked, probably knowing I hadn't.

"I was up that way and kind of got diverted."

"No worries. I heard about your afternoon. The boss had a smile on his face that could have cracked his makeup on his way out the door."

"What did you find?" I changed the subject as quickly as I

could, not wanting to revisit the visual of Martinez applying his makeup.

"They treated a woman."

"Did you get a name?"

"I tried, but they all hide behind that HIPAA law thing. Said we needed a warrant for them to divulge personal information."

I already knew the name. Susan McLeash lived in the vicinity of the clinic.

26

Could Susan McLeash kill someone? The question was running on a continuous loop in my head. I decided that, despite all her defects, our girl was a train wreck, not a cold-blooded killer. Robinson was in my sights, but I was wary of confronting him until I had some hard evidence. Martinez's warning about treading lightly around another agency was a rare pearl of wisdom from him. Susan was another story. I had no problem confronting her. The list of questions was growing as fast as the evidence to her involvement. My head was spinning a half-hour later when I pulled up to her condo.

If we were to have any kind of candid conversation, I needed to surprise her. She was too accomplished a liar for me to give her any time to fabricate her answers. It was a crapshoot if she'd be home on a Friday around happy hour, but I had nothing else.

I knew I might be treading water and killing time until one or both of the fishermen were arrested, but I still wanted answers. I already knew Robinson was involved, but not to what extent. The best-case scenario for taking him down was if one of the fishermen rolled on him. Thinking about those two, I picked up my phone and texted Grace, asking if they had been apprehended. It was a long shot, at least this close in time to the incident. They had headed toward the river after dumping the body and likely had docked the boat. With the video of the rescue going viral, there was a good chance they had seen it and taken off. It made sense for them to go inland. There might be a lot of water here, but with radar and the shaky condition of their boat, there were few places to hide.

Without waiting for an answer, I took a deep breath, left the protection of the truck, and crossed no-man's land, reaching Susan's door without taking any fire from the enemy. Breathing in again, I rang the bell and waited.

"Just a minute. You're early!" she called out from inside.

Last night was still fresh in my mind, but she had apparently moved on and was ready for more action. A few seconds later, I heard the click-clack of heels on the tile floor and the door opened.

"Oh, Kurt." The disappointment was evident. "What are you doing here?"

"Hello, Susan. We need to talk, and I thought it would be better to do it in private."

"Well, your timing sucks." She looked past me, scanning the street for whoever she was expecting.

I wasn't in the mood for her games. "It'll just take a second."

She knew her best chance was to get rid of me before her date showed up. Opening the door enough to let me in, she shot another glance at the street before closing the door behind me.

What stood in front of me was nothing I wanted to see. I'd have a hard time forgetting it.

Her skin-tight leather pants bulged in all the wrong places, which the low-cut, too-tight blouse was supposed to distract you from—and failed. Fortunately, she had chosen to leave the shirt untucked. Her makeup did little to cover her cross-eyed look. Averting my gaze, I tried to remember why I was here.

"Last Sunday. Where were you around three?"

"Would that be A.M. or P.M.?" she snarled. "You looking for me to give you an alibi, Hunter?"

I might have had the element of surprise, but she was still quick with her retort. "Your truck was at headquarters at the time of the murder. It's in the security video."

Her eyes crossed even more as she thought back. "I was here. Saturday night was kind of a rough one. Slept most of the day on Sunday."

I could only imagine what a bender she must have been on to sleep all day. I had seen her pretty much obliterated on many occasions and still make it into work the next morning.

"This is important, Susan. How did your truck get there?" I did my best to make it seem like I was on her side.

She shrugged, causing her breasts to lift. "I don't know."

I scolded myself for looking, but unfortunately, what has been seen cannot be unseen. This might have been the first honest answer she had given. "Who were you with Saturday night?"

She fought hard to hold back the first tear. As it streaked down her face, leaving a trail through her makeup, others followed, creating a deep trough.

"Can I get a drink?"

If you called breaking a woman down a victory, I had just hit a home run. It didn't make me feel any better, and I nodded. She turned and walked to the kitchen. Scanning for defects in the cheap paint on the hallway walls to avoid looking at her, I followed. With practiced movements, she pulled a Tervis cup from a cabinet and filled it with ice from the dispenser on the freezer-side door of the refrigerator, moved to another cabinet, pulled out a half-full bottle of Kettle One vodka, unscrewed the cap, and poured a healthy dollop over the ice.

"Want anything?" she asked.

"Maybe some juice or water? Have to meet my daughter soon." It was an easy excuse for not drinking with her. She nodded toward the refrigerator and took a healthy sip of her drink.

As I opened the refrigerator, I couldn't help but notice there were no pictures, clippings, or notes on the door. A refrigerator is a good indicator of how someone lives their life. The interior was empty as well, save for a partially consumed twelve-pack, some bread, and a pill container. Squinting at the label, it appeared to be an antibiotic. The empty fridge door was interesting as well. Some excessive neat-freaks banned magnets on their refrigerators. A glance around the messy kitchen confirmed she wasn't one of those. I felt a little sorry that the outside was as empty as the inside.

Taking my glass, I filled it with water from the dispenser. She had moved to the bar, where she sat, drink in her hand, and tears streaking her face. I moved across from her and leaned against the lower counter.

"Look. I can help you if you tell me what's going on. I've got to tell you, the evidence shows you're involved." I didn't feel the need to tell her every detail—she knew.

"Oh, Kurt. I was really starting to like Derek. He was nice to me, took me to fancy restaurants and shopping." She paused to take another sip. "But then they started saying bad things about him."

The entire week I had been calling Hayward by his last name. It was strange to hear her say his first. "Who did?"

"Mostly Jim Scott. He even started making threats." She lifted the glass, swirled the ice cubes, and polished it off. Rising, she moved across the kitchen and refilled the glass. While she had her back to me, I checked my watch, realizing I was going to be late to meet Allie. I thought about texting her, but I couldn't afford to distract Susan. Her refill consisted of pouring more vodka into the glass. There was no need for ice. Between the insulation in the cup and the speed with which she finished the drink, it had hardly melted.

I watched her as she returned to the stool and sat down. She was pretty much outright crying now, and I was glad for the two feet of cheap granite barrier separating us that limited the amount of comfort she could expect. The façade Susan used in her daily life had fallen away, revealing a twelve-year-old in a woman's body.

I was getting where I needed to be with her, and knowing I was going to be late to meet Allie, I pushed. "What did Robinson do?"

"Scott threatened him, too. Said as the boss he was responsible for what his employees did."

I already knew Scott's story. I dug deeper into Robinson's. "I guess he didn't take that too well."

"I tried to stand up for him and Derek, but Scott started getting angry. He wanted to fight. Two of the other guys dragged him outside."

That left Susan alone with Robinson and Hayward. "What happened then?"

"Robinson went to get us another round. While he was gone, I asked Derek if what Scott said was true." She stopped to drink again.

"And?"

"Then he got really defensive and we got in a fight. I got up to leave and he grabbed me, showing me this lobster-gauge thing. Trying to tell me that it was all legit. This whole thing sounded like it was getting too close to home for me. I can't afford to endanger my job to protect those guys playing games with fishermen and stuff right by the park."

Self-preservation was our girl's top priority. The drink sat empty in front of her. She was rolling now, her eyes were dry, and the previous emotion was gone from her voice.

"I reached for the gauge, you know, to check it out, and Derek got all freaked out and pulled it back. Cut the crap out of me." She rolled up her sleeve and showed me a bandage on her arm. "I got up to find something to stop the bleeding. He must have thought I was leaving, but I was just heading to the restroom to clean up. Then he grabbed me for real."

"What'd you do?"

"Robinson stepped in and took me outside. He thought I'd had too much to drink and didn't want me to drive, so he took me home."

"What'd he drive?" I was almost rooting for her to give me the answer that would exonerate her.

"We took my truck. He said something about coming to the bar with one of the guys that had taken Scott home." She thought for a minute, using the downtime to take another sip. "Scott and the two other guys were gone by then."

The evidence against Susan explained, I started to leave when the doorbell rang. I turned and asked her, "Do you think Robinson could have killed Hayward to cover up what they were doing?"

Before she could answer the doorbell rang again. I saw the panicked look on her face and solved the dilemma for her.

"I'll wait till you're gone and let myself out."

She grabbed my arm. "Thanks, Kurt, owe you one."

It would have been almost a touching gesture if she hadn't winked. Badly wanting to see who her date was, I waited a second, then followed her into the hall and slid into the closet. Leaving the door cracked, I immediately felt a sneeze coming on from the miasma of perfume on the clothes. Holding my breath, I tickled the roof of my mouth with my tongue, hoping to subvert it, while I looked out into the hallway.

Susan opened the front door and a man stepped in.

The sneeze almost escaped my nose, but I choked it back, surprised when I saw the captain of the fishing boat step in. He was dressed in shorts and a t-shirt, not clothes for a date. Her face showed the same disappointed look I had seen when she opened the door for me. She was clearly expecting someone else.

"He sent me to pick you up. You ready?" the captain asked.

Susan grabbed her bag from a chair by the door and they left. The second the door closed, I left the protection of the closet and moved quickly down the hallway. I reached the window just as a red pickup pulled away from the curb. Rewinding my memory, I tried to recall if the red truck had been in the lot at the time of Hayward's murder, but came up blank. Last night he had driven away in an old beater. This was a newer model, with a lift kit and detailing. Either truck was recognizable. I needed to check Martinez's video to see if Robinson had enlisted the captain's help, as he had with Scott; but this time, to kill Hayward.

What I should have done, and what I did, were two separate things. With a BOLO out on the man already, my duty was to call Miami-Dade dispatch, but I was torn, not wanting to implicate Susan, who at this point appeared to be in the clear. At the same time, I wanted more evidence if he was tied to Hayward's murder as well. Unlike Robinson, I had witnessed firsthand that the captain was capable of killing someone. It was too late to follow the truck, but I needed to do something, so I called Grace.

"Should have got the tag number and called it in, Hunter."

I didn't blame her for sounding angry. Instead of apologizing, I gave her Susan's address, a description of the truck, and the direction they were heading. Grace disconnected, saying she would handle it, leaving me standing in Susan's hallway, powerless. Checking my watch, I realized I wasn't late yet, but with the half-hour drive, I would be. The logical thing to do was to let Miami-Dade handle it and head back to headquarters to meet my daughter and her friend.

Instead, I left Susan's house, hopped in my truck, and took off in the direction I had seen the red pickup head.

27

STEVEN BECKER
A KURT HUNTER MYSTERY
BACKWATER FLATS

It was likely a futile effort, but with the help of the police scanner I was able to follow the chase. My thoughts went to Susan. She was a wild card for sure and a certifiable pain, but she was a coworker, and appeared to be guilty of nothing more than being a fool. With the red pickup unaware, at least at this point, that it was a target, I followed the well-coordinated efforts of the Miami-Dade police. I was cognizant of my location and Allie's ETA. The red pickup was moving south. Currently in Kendall, I could reach headquarters fairly quickly and decided to follow the chase until Allie called.

When my phone dinged with a message from Allie that they were pulling into the parking lot, I quickly changed course. Making a quick U-turn, I headed south to headquarters, leaving the chase to Miami-Dade. At the first red light, I texted Allie that I was on the way and got a smiley face emoji in return.

Turning down the volume on the scanner, I headed back to the turnpike. The Friday exodus from Miami changed my status from a little late to very late. The expected twenty-minute trip had doubled. Heading east, traffic continued to be heavy for the first mile until the development tapered off. I found my speed drifting north of seventy as I listened to the chatter on the scanner. It wasn't as compelling as some chases, but as the dragnet closed in on the red pickup, I started to feel the excitement of a predator just before he strikes his prey. Then the road quickly degraded to a pot-holed mess, adding several more minutes to my tardiness. Finally, I made the turn into the parking lot at headquarters and looked for Allie.

Pulling out my phone to call her, I saw a message I had missed. The notification must have been obscured by the noise from the scanner.

"We got a lift to your house," it read.

My first thought was that Ray had found the girls, but as I walked to the marina, I saw the twin-engine FWC boat was gone. With Hayward dead, and Scott terminated, that left only Robinson as possible pilot.

There was little chance that Robinson had seen me when he handed off Scott to the fishermen earlier. He was long gone before I entered the water. What I hadn't counted on was a viral video of the rescue. My advantage was now a liability—a serious one, if Robinson had seen the video.

Running to my boat, I jumped aboard and pulled out my phone. Scrolling through my messages from Martinez, I found the one with the list of MMSI numbers. I zoomed in on the RHIB and punched the number into my VHF. There was no response, and I racked my brain for any other way to track him. Martinez was long gone from the office, probably standing at attention behind a podium somewhere telling the world, or anyone who would listen, how great he and the park service were—in that order.

A boat coming into the marina caught my attention. Johnny Wells and his Interceptor were pulling in. The quad outboards hanging from his transom would help, but what I really wanted was his radar. Running back toward the seawall at the side of the marina, I stood by his slip ready to receive the dock lines as he idled in.

"Yo, Kurt. Thanks, man."

"Not a courtesy call. I need your help."

"Sure thing, man, we were just calling it a day."

A day for the Interceptor probably meant several hundred miles of high-speed action. I meant to add only another dozen, if he was willing.

"I don't have time to tell the story, but I think my daughter's in trouble."

"No worries. Drop the line and jump on." I heard him ask his crew if they were up for a quick run.

Releasing the line, I ran to the side of the boat adjacent to the dock and jumped onto the gunwale, then down to the deck. Carefully manipulating the twin controls, Johnny was backing out of the slip as I reached the helm. With two engines on each control plus a bow thruster, he had plenty of maneuverability, and had spun a one-eighty in the footprint of the boat.

"Where to?" he asked as he pushed the throttles forward.

"Adams Key for a start. Hoping we can locate someone on your radar."

"What are we looking at?"

"The FWC RHIB."

"That old boy actually took it out?" I caught his skeptical look. And as he pushed the boat to the maximum speed he could get away with in the channel leading to the bay, I explained what had happened. The sense of urgency of both him and his crew ratcheted up a notch as we scanned the radar. Zooming the ring out to ten miles, there were too many possible targets. To make matters worse, the radar could not separate items adjacent to each other. The landmass of the islands absorbed any boats against them.

"You gotta give me a timeline or something. Nice Friday afternoons got 'em all out."

I thought for a second, and pulled my phone out. Scanning the messages, I found the one from Allie that they had gotten a ride to my house and checked the timestamp.

"They would have left the park forty minutes ago," I answered, cursing myself that true confessions at Susan McLeash's and my decision to hang with the police chase had endangered my daughter—and her friend.

"Even with that knuckle-dragger at the helm, that sucker can fly," Johnny reminded me.

The boating conditions were stellar, giving even more range to the RHIB. Figuring he'd be running at thirty to forty knots, that would put him about twenty miles out by now. As we idled out the channel, all I could do was try and get into his head. He knew I was more familiar with the backwaters of the bay than he was, so I didn't think he would try to hide in the park.

I had to set my emotional involvement aside, and I asked myself what his motive was. Thoughts spun through my head, all of them bad. I decided to find him first and ask questions later.

"I think he'd be on the outside."

Johnny increased the zoom to its maximum. "The outer band is thirty miles. Its range is thirty-six. You're not going to see much ocean-side with the islands blocking the signal."

"Let's head out Caesar Creek, then."

Johnny nodded, nursing the controls until we passed the fuel dock. From here we could see the channel was clear. Hitting the switch for the light bar, he eased the throttles to their stops. Powered by the four, 300-horsepower engines, the boat took off like a rocket. We were up on plane, skipping over the tops of the waves, in the time it would have taken my boat to accelerate.

Easing back the throttles, he settled the engines in at 4400 rpms and adjusted the trim. The GPS showed our cruising speed approaching sixty knots. With nothing to do until we covered some miles, I tried to control my boat envy and focus on my daughter.

Adams Key came into sight some five minutes later, and another five after that we were about to fly past and enter Caesar Creek, when I saw two boats at the dock. Ray's was one and the twin-engine FWC, with Robinson's bulk at the helm, was the other. I frantically searched for Allie and her friend. They weren't aboard or on the dock, but a second later, I saw them on the grass playing with Zero.

Robinson was just about to push off when the wake from the Interceptor hit the dock. As I ducked behind the large console, I saw him grab the dock with one hand and flip off Johnny and his crew with the other. The Interceptor was running too fast to execute a turn before reaching the creek, forcing us to proceed through it and make our turn on the Atlantic side. By the time we circled back the RHIB was gone.

"Allie!" I yelled as we approached the dock.

"Dad, what are you doing on that boat?"

"You know Johnny and the guys."

She walked over and said hello to the captain, who had performed Justine's and my wedding ceremony. "You guys okay?"

"Hey, Mr. Hunter," Allie's friend greeted me.

"Dad, this is Lana."

"Cool boat," she said.

My boat envy started anew. "Unfortunately, I was just getting a ride. What's with Robinson bringing you over?"

Allie shrugged. She had no idea what I had been going through for the last half-hour. "You were late, and he offered."

"That was nice of him." She was a little too old to give the "don't take rides from strangers" talk. Besides, he was essentially a coworker. There was no way for her to know he was the lead suspect in a murder investigation.

"You guys good? I'll get a ride back to headquarters with Johnny and bring the boat back." I checked my watch. "Justine probably won't get here for another few hours."

"Can we ride on that?" Allie asked. Her friend crowded behind her as they gawked at the Interceptor—and the crew.

I glanced at Johnny, who nodded. The girls saw his acknowledgment and without waiting for the words to come out of my mouth hopped aboard, leaving Zero staring at us and pouting.

"We'll be back in a few," I told him. His stump of a tail wagged as he plopped down on the dock to wait.

With the girls standing on either side of Johnny, I was relegated to the collapsible bench in front of the transom for the trip back. Unlike the balls-to-the-wall trip out, this ride was more of a pleasure cruise; the boat settled in nicely at forty knots instead of the sixty we'd been running before. It was a comfortable ride and probably saved the taxpayers a wad of cash at the same time. Even with the efficiency of the new engines, twelve hundred horsepower, running flat out, will drain a gas tank at the rate of about fifty gallons an hour. I knew I'd been working for Martinez for too long when I figured using the Interceptor for the ride out cost over a hundred bucks.

The calculations didn't last long and I started thinking about Robinson. Under normal circumstances—normal being defined as a week ago, or before Hayward was killed—there was no way he would have offered the girls a ride. That left two options: He was trying to be nice and help me out, or it was an attempt to scare me. The latter was the sure bet.

The Interceptor was back in the channel again, and I looked up, surprised to see Allie at the wheel. I shook my head, aware that life as I knew it had just ended. The only thing in my favor was that we had already passed the fuel dock and I didn't need to see, or worry about paying, the fuel bill. Slipping into the channel, Johnny took control and eased the boat into its spot on the dock.

"Appreciate you running me out there." I wasn't going to thank him for letting Allie drive the mid-six-figure boat.

"Hey, no worries. I would have freaked out too if that son of a bitch had my girl."

I caught a glance from Allie, who must have heard the comment. She left it alone for now, not wanting to embarrass her friend, who was chatting up the crew. We exchanged a look unique to fathers and daughters—when we returned to the island, I figured we'd be having a chat. The crew started to hose down the Interceptor and I thanked Johnny again before heading over to the park service boat. After riding on the Interceptor, it seemed even smaller than before, and as the three of us idled out of the marina, we each looked over at the sleek ICE cruiser with envy.

28

If Robinson's intention was to scare me, he had succeeded in the short term; but now that I knew the girls were safe, what he had done was to fill my tank with resolve. I'd been avoiding a confrontation until I had more evidence—that had all changed now. My problem was that for the time being I was in charge of two teenage girls, and after what had just happened, I wasn't going to let them out of my sight. Justine was about two hours out, requiring me to come up with an activity. Otherwise we'd end up sitting around and staring at each other.

"You guys want to fish or snorkel?" I'd told Allie during the week that it wouldn't be fair to her friend if we dove and left her alone on the boat.

"Allie said we could maybe find some lobsters," Lana said.

Perfect. "Sure thing. Why don't you guys get changed and I'll load the boat? And make sure Lana gets a license with a lobster stamp. You can do it online." After everything that had happened this week, the last thing I wanted to do was promote unlicensed activity.

From the small storage closet under the house I pulled out three sets of snorkeling gear, tickle sticks, and nets. The plastic gauges attached to the sticks caught my eye, reminding me that I was playing hooky while a murderer was running free. I'd had this conversation with myself before, as well as with Justine. Law enforcement officers are entitled to time off, especially if there was no threat to someone's life. I was after a murderer, not a serial killer. The distinction was a big one, but didn't help me relax. Figuring after I got Allie and Lana in the water, I'd check in on the chase, I loaded the boat and waited for the girls.

They appeared a few minutes later, wearing rash guards over their swimsuits, the long sleeves being essential protection against the coral. Heading out Caesar Creek, I found a nice grouping of coral heads in eight feet of water. Pulling past them, I dropped the anchor in the sand and let the boat swing until the transom was behind and to the side of the area, making it easier for the girls to return to the boat. Allie gave Lana a brief and pretty funny simulation of how to trap a lobster, then helped her with her mask and snorkel. While they finished getting ready, I put up the dive flag. A few minutes later the girls were in the water.

There was little to do now except keep an eye on them, and watch for any boaters ignorant of the warning flag. With an hour before the sunset, the water was quiet, and it was easy to watch the girls as they kicked around on the surface.

I had checked the scanner and radio. The pickup had eluded the pursuit. That result left me deep in thought about Robinson and his actions; it was only this morning that he'd delivered a subdued Scott to the fishermen and an hour ago he had—or at least showed me he could—abduct my daughter. I had to wonder what was next.

A scream broke the spell and I jumped to my feet. Allie was kicking hard to the boat with Lana a few yards behind her.

"We found a ghost trap!"

The sea floor was littered with old anchors, gear, and traps. It was unfortunate when the lines holding the marking buoys were cut, usually by propellers. Because of this, the fish, lobster, and crab traps all had built-in "escape" panels that allowed the sea life its freedom after a period of time. To a recreational diver, finding a ghost trap, especially one that was fresh in the water was gold. "How long's it been down?"

"Looks pretty new," she said.

She and Lana kicked back to the spot they'd found it. Over the next fifteen minutes they went up and down, working the lobsters out of the trap, and bringing them over to the boat one at a time. As soon as they hit the deck, I measured them with one of my gauges and, finding them all legal sized, dropped them into the live well.

"There's still one more!" Allie yelled. She took a deep breath and dropped under the surface.

I was helping Lana with her fins and didn't notice when Allies' head broke the surface.

"There's something else in there," she called.

From her tone, I could tell it wasn't a lobster. Looking over at her, I saw only a whirlpool, evidence of where Allie had dived back down.

"Do you know what she found?" I asked Lana as I helped her aboard.

"Nope. But did you see them all?"

"Nice catch." She was expecting some kind of celebratory gesture; I wasn't sure what to do with her, and decided on a fist bump.

Allie was back on the surface.

"What do you have?" I asked her.

"There's a bag in the trap. I can't get it out." She spoke in gasps, trying to refill her lungs at the same time as explaining to me what she found.

Checking her position against the wind and current, I yelled back that I could move the boat. I went to the bow, where I started feeding out anchor line. The boat drifted back to within a few feet of where Allie was treading water.

"Should I come in or should we pull it?"

"I think we have to pull it."

"Hold on, I'll get a line." The depth was just over the length of a single dock line, so I hooked two together using one of the braided eyes, sliding it into the other, then back through itself. Pulling the line tight, I tossed it to Allie. Lana and I were both at the transom watching her as she took several deep breaths and submerged. It seemed like she was down a long time, but I could see her working below.

"What do you think it is?" Lana asked.

I held back the first answer that came to my mind. A package in the water in South Florida usually meant drugs. A weapon was my second guess, and that wasn't much better.

Before I could answer, Allie surfaced. She hung by the ladder and handed me the end of the line. I followed it into the water and crossed to the starboard side to get a better angle before hauling it in. Hand over hand, I brought the trap up until it was just at the surface. I could see a sealed dry bag floating in the trap. With a bag of concrete poured in the bottom, the traps weighed over sixty pounds, almost impossible to lift from the water without the aid of a winch. Even holding the weight of it was difficult. I tied the line off to a cleat and caught my breath.

"Can you open the lid?" I asked Allie, who was still in the water.

She swam over to the trap and started to mess with the latch. "I tried down there." I watched as she pulled against the lid. Someone had fastened it shut. I looked around the boat and eyed the fire extinguisher attached to the console.

Grabbing it, I returned to the transom. "Look out," I called to Allie. "You too, Lana."

I waited until both girls were clear, adjusted my sunglasses to protect my eyes, and slammed the base of the cylinder into the trap. The thin boards shattered and I reached inside, pulling the bag out. With no way to bring the trap aboard, I used a fender, tying it to the line before releasing the trap-line tied to the cleat. The trap fell quickly to the bottom. I wasn't sure if marking the location was necessary. Depending on what was in the bag, it might or might not be evidence.

As I tried to decide the best way to handle it, both girls gathered around as I looked at the bag. With Justine's voice in my head, I fought my urge to see immediately what was inside and took several pictures first. Next, I pulled on a pair of nitrile gloves, and conducted a visual examination. If it were evidence found on land, I would have been more cautious, but the seawater would have eradicated any trace of fingerprints or DNA on the exterior of the bag.

Unopened, it was impossible to determine the contents of the bag, though I guessed it to be lighter than a gun—much lighter. Whatever was inside needed to be handled with care. Protected from the elements, the contents hopefully would be covered with fingerprints and DNA.

With Allie looking over my port shoulder, and Lana my starboard, I released the clasp, and unrolled the top of the bag, which broke the seal, releasing the air contained inside. Carefully, I opened the bag and peered inside. As I did, I could feel the girls behind me as they pressed closer to get a look.

Unable to see inside, I reached into the bag. It was mostly empty—except for a rigid object on the bottom. Slowly, not knowing what it was or how fragile it might be, I grasped it gently and removed it.

That the mystery object was just a lobster gauge was anticlimactic for the girls, who expected something more obviously gruesome, but they didn't know, as I did, that the dried blood on it was from Officer Hayward.

This was not the time to examine it further. I placed the gauge back in the bag, and sealed it, before carefully putting it in the cooler.

"You guys want to run to Miami?" I asked.

"Are we going to the crime lab?" Allie asked.

"If it's good with Justine." I picked up my phone and called. The girls hovered around me, their excitement evident when she agreed. "We'll run up to the condo and she'll pick us up there."

"How cool is that!" Allie said, more to Lana than to me.

With the fender marking the trap, I called Ray to see if he would help retrieve it. After reading the coordinates of the location and describing the fender, he promised he would grab it for me.

The girls and I then quickly sorted and stored the gear. The lobsters were still in the live well, but there was nothing to be done about that now, as we had no ice. Once we got to Miami, we would have to deal with their disposition. I started the engine and, with Allie at the wheel, went to the bow and pulled the anchor, then returned to the helm and studied the chartplotter. I knew the waters well enough to not need its assistance, but there was a detour I wanted to make. We usually took the inside route, but instead, I took over the wheel and pointed the bow to the northeast, and the open waters of the Atlantic.

Allie and Lana were forward, sitting together on the built-in cooler in front of the console. I couldn't hear them, but they were clearly excited about the lobsters, the find, and now a trip to the crime lab. Once past Elliott Key, I continued past Sands and Boca Chita Keys. From there, the barrier islands became smaller, some barely visible at low tide; most not visible at all. In order to avoid the hazards I turned further east.

In the distance I could see the Cape Florida Lighthouse, but I had to navigate past Stiltsville first. Staying clear of the remaining decrepit stilt structures built on the shoals south of Key Biscayne, I automatically scanned the area around the iconic houses, looking for trouble. The once-popular water-based community had been built in the 1920s to circumvent some of the land-based laws: prohibition, gambling, and whoring, to name a few. These days what was left of the village harbored illicit activity.

The disposition of Stiltsville was one of the few things Martinez and I agreed on. The park's boundaries had been extended some years ago to encompass the area. He loathed the maintenance implications on his budget, and I, the trouble the area brought. If it were torn down, we would both be happier.

I followed the coast of Key Biscayne, giving the shallows around its northern end plenty of room, before making a turn for the bridge across Bear Cut. I was shocked when I saw the old fishing boat anchored under the same span as last night. I couldn't tell how many people were aboard. And that led me to wonder what had happened to Susan McLeash. Apparently, at least one of the fishermen hadn't gotten the memo that there was a BOLO out for them, and Miami-Dade, thinking they'd fled inland, wasn't looking out here.

Dropping my speed slightly to navigate through the pilings, we reached the bay side without incident. Once clear of any obstructions, I turned for the main span of the Rickenbacker Causeway, and called Grace Herrera.

29

Just as we reached the crime lab, I received a text from Grace that the fishermen had been taken into custody. I responded, asking if Susan had been with them. The answer came back negative.

For a brief second, I wondered if I shouldn't have requested Miami-Dade check the water under the boat. Susan's whereabouts were unknown, and the last person she'd been seen with was the captain. I'd already witnessed him dump one body today. I recalled him saying when he picked Susan up that he was taking her to meet someone, and hoped that was the case.

There's a feeling I get when a case is about to wrap up. That doesn't mean everything is going to be neat and tidy, but between the lobster gauge in the dry bag and the fishermen in custody, it certainly seemed like my investigation was coming to a head. For all the legitimate detective work that I had done, it appeared that taking Allie and her friend lobstering might have provided the smoking gun.

Justine met us at the door and, after exchanging hugs with Allie and introducing Lana, we headed back to the lab. It was close to eight o'clock on a Friday, and the lab was deserted.

Wanting to know if the gauge would tell me who the killer was, I pushed Justine to give Lana the abbreviated tour. I caught a couple of looks, but Allie had been through this before, and was itching to see if her find helped solve one of my cases.

"Alright, kemosabe, let's see what we've got here." Justine held up the bag and inspected the exterior.

I bit my lip, knowing I better be patient or she wouldn't hesitate to toss me out. Allie and Lana hung onto every word and action as she finally removed the metal piece from the bag.

"Can we check if it's a legal one or not?" I asked.

Her eyes burned through me, and I knew I had overstepped my bounds. Everything she did, from receiving evidence to appearing in court, was based on procedure. She would get to it when she got to it.

In the meantime, I stepped aside and called Grace, asking her to send over the fingerprints of the fishermen as soon as they were processed. She was more than happy to comply. The arrest was a gift and, in addition to the attempted murder they already had been booked on, if one of them turned out to be Hayward's killer, she would get a good deal of the credit.

Moving back to Justine's work area, I noticed a ruler on the table alongside the gauge. Peering over Allie's shoulder, it looked like the gap between the two points was three inches—a legal gauge.

That changed the equation. The killer was someone who had discovered the scam, and was not part of it—or at least not the procuring part. If I was right, that eliminated Robinson—and Susan. They both knew about the rigged gauges. The fishermen knew nothing except that the lobster they were buying were legal size. I doubted they gave a thought or care to where they came from, or how they were obtained. Scott moved back into the lead of suspects, and I texted Grace to see if he was still in the hospital.

"My money's on Scott's fingerprints being on the gauge," I said to Justine.

Finally, I had said something that didn't get daggers shot at me. Instead, it was pointed sarcasm.

"And, Detective, what makes you think that?"

"It's a legal gauge. Whoever killed Hayward didn't know about the scam."

"Scott thought they were confiscating shorts?" she asked.

"Dudley Do Right, is what they call him. There's a good chance, yeah."

"Well, let's have a look-see."

Justine took the gauge to a glass-enclosed unit and placed it inside. After pressing a switch, the unit sent a stream of powder into the case, allowed it to settle, and then sucked out the remainder. When it cleared, several fingerprints were clearly visible on the gauge.

"There ya go," Justine said, removing the metal piece from the machine. "I'll start running them now."

"No need." While she had been working on the gauge, Grace had sent over the booking records for the fishermen. I handed her my phone. "That's the two fishermen, and we have Scott's prints here already. I'm betting it matches one of them."

"Right on, Sherlock," she said.

Allie and Lana giggled at the barb while Justine carried the gauge back to her workstation. The prints on my phone were no use to her, but she had digital access to the records. She scanned the prints on the gauge.

"How long does it take?" Allie asked.

It was good to see two teenage girls interested in something besides their phones. "The longer it has to search, the less likely there's a match," Allie said.

"You've been watching too much CSI: Miami," Justine said. "You need between twelve and twenty points in common for it to be a match. The program works through the entire print, either way."

A few seconds later we had our answer, and it wasn't the one I was looking for. *No Match* appeared in large capital letters on the screen.

"Any other bright ideas?" Justine asked.

"Robinson and Susan." There was no one left.

"The only thing Susan McLeash can premeditate is her next drink. She didn't kill him."

The girls giggled again, but Justine was correct. It was looking like Robinson had set up Susan. Scott must have found out and hid the evidence. Blackmail as a motive came to mind. "Susan's a federal employee, her prints are easy, but I'll have to get Robinson's."

"There might be an easier way. If Scott wasn't the killer, maybe he planted the bag." Justine picked up the dry bag and started to examine it.

After carefully checking the folds, especially where it rolled over on itself to make the seal, she took it back to the print machine and placed it inside. We waited for the smoke to clear. Several partial prints were visible.

"It won't be enough for court, but that's not what we're after." She took the bag back to her workstation and scanned the prints.

A minute later the screen indicated a match: Jim Scott.

"Can you hang out with the girls for a bit? I have to make a social call."

"You guys want pizza?" Justine asked.

She was already a rock star in their eyes; this just added to it. I said goodbye, and we made plans to meet later on at Adams Key. Justine would take them back in our boat, and I would follow in the park service center console. If there was a way to wrap this up tonight, I was going to do it.

Heading out to Justine's car, I entered Jackson Memorial Hospital into the maps app. Mindlessly following the computerized voice giving me directions, I was looking forward to what Jim Scott had to say, and wondered if it would match the narrative running through my head. At least the fishermen were in custody, I had at least until tomorrow morning before they were arraigned. With the charge of attempted murder of a law enforcement officer hanging over their heads, the bail was likely to be substantial. If I needed them, I had a pretty good idea where they'd be.

As I pulled up to the hospital, I hoped my distaste for Robinson wasn't clouding my judgment.

Grace had texted me the room number, allowing me to bypass the reception deck and head directly for the elevators. Rehearsing the questions on my way to the room, I heard voices and stopped outside. Before I entered, I could hear Scott trying to talk someone into releasing him. I quickly stepped in, to see if I could convince him that this was the safest place for him right now. If he was planning a jailbreak, I aimed to put a stop to it.

"The tests are negative, but we'd like to keep you overnight for observation," the doctor said.

"I'm fine—really."

I could hear the frustration in both their voices and wondered how long the conversation had been going on.

"Hey, how're you feeling?" I asked as I entered.

"Hunter, tell them to let me go."

That was the last thing I wanted to do. Instead, I flashed my credentials at the doctor and asked if I could have a few minutes alone with his patient. He seemed relieved, and quickly left, asking me to have the nurse station page him when I was finished. Scott's bed was the closest to the door of the twin room. The curtain was drawn around the other space. Before saying anything, I checked to make sure it was vacant.

"I can't speak from a health perspective, but I think you should spend the night." Our brief talk before he left in the ambulance was nowhere close to a statement. I figured he might be able to fill in some of the blanks. Sitting in the chair by the bed, I pulled out my notepad and phone. "You okay if I record this?"

"I already gave Miami-Dade a statement."

"I'm thinking this might cover some different ground."

"Do what you need to. I just want to be done with this whole charade."

There was no thank you for saving his life, just his usual righteous indignation. I picked up the phone, opened the voice memo app, and pressed *Record*. After going through the preliminary information: date, time, location, name ... I asked him to confirm he had consented to the recording.

"Just get on with it," he snapped.

I figured I might as well start our chat by tossing a grenade. "I found your stash."

His expression told me he was going into denial mode. I threw the facts out there before he could say anything. "The dry bag had your prints on the fold. The gauge is being processed as we speak." Wanting to see how he handled himself, I didn't tell him I already knew the results.

"Son of a bitch," he muttered.

The room was silent for a few long seconds while he decided how to proceed. In no rush, I leaned back in the chair and waited. Even if you were trained in the tactic and knew it was being used against you, remaining silent was a powerful method to get someone talking.

"I guess I owe you for saving me. Did they get those pricks that tossed me?"

"They were arrested a few hours ago."

"That's a start."

"How about you tell me why Robinson wanted you dead? The fishermen will be charged with attempted murder; Robinson was merely an accomplice, and I'm the only witness."

Suddenly, Robinson's taking the girls earlier made sense. If I was under his thumb, there was nothing to tie him to the attempt on Scott's life. Even if the fishermen testified, I wasn't sure anyone would believe them. I wondered if I should tell Justine what had happened with Robinson and the girls. At least for now, they were safe in the lab. I'd wait until Justine texted that they were leaving before deciding what precautions to take.

"I'd watch that son of a bitch if I were you," Scott said, reading my mind.

"The story—" I was getting anxious now, and thinking twice about leaving Justine to take Allie and Lana back to Adams Key.

"Alright already." Scott tugged on his IV, as if he wanted to pull it out and run.

I leaned forward, sensing the moment of truth was coming.

"I needed something to hold over his head. Those guys were threatening more than my job. I just wanted them to stop selling the shorts—until I found out about the rigged gauges."

"Walk me through what happened after your shift last Sunday."

"We had this big blow-up Saturday night. It was about to go to fisticuffs when a couple of the guys dragged me out of the bar. I decided at that point that I needed to protect myself."

"So, you witnessed a murder and hid the weapon to blackmail the killer?" Now that my theory was playing out, I was getting even more concerned about Justine and the girls. Then I remembered that Susan was in the wind as well.

"Something like that. I have no doubt that if I turned Robinson in, he would have implicated me in their side business. Nothing like having a boss looking out for your interests."

"I wouldn't know." Martinez and I seldom got along, but I

would never hold something on him to make my life easier. "If you think your exposure is limited to concealing evidence, you're dead wrong." I wasn't going to tell him that his actions could be endangering my family.

"Give me a second, I've gotta make a call." Picking up my phone, I paused the recording and stepped out of the room.

Once out of earshot, I called Grace, filled her in on what Scott had done, and asked her to place him under guard. I wasn't sure what charge to hold him on, but the DA could handle that. She placed me on hold. Before she came back on the line, I saw a Miami-Dade officer approaching.

"You Hunter?"

"That was fast. He's in there."

"There's another inmate on this floor. My partner's keeping an eye on him. Is this guy a threat?"

"I don't think so. The doctor wants to hold him overnight for observation. That'll buy me enough time to figure out what to charge him with."

"Okay, I got it." The officer handed me a card with his cell number written on the back. "Just let me know if anything changes. I'll make sure he doesn't check out AMA."

30

STEVEN BECKER
A KURT HUNTER MYSTERY
BACKWATER FLATS

I DIDN'T WALK OUT OF THE HOSPITAL—I RAN. BY THE TIME I reached Justine's car, the combination of my anxiety and the South Florida heat and humidity had coated my skin with sweat. Starting the car, I configured the AC vents to hit my face, placed the unit on maximum and sped out of the parking lot.

As soon as I hit the street, I called Justine. The ringing was interminable until the call went to voicemail. That could mean several things: she was still at work, or she couldn't hear the phone over the boat's engine. I didn't want to consider the last option: Robinson.

Somehow, he had a knack of staying in front of this situation, even if it meant killing someone. With no regard for the speed limit—a condition in which I was not alone—I arrived at the crime lab and called Justine again. Voicemail. I texted Allie, and after a long pause my phone dinged. Whew. Asking her to let me in, I ran to the entrance and waited.

We were all together now, and that's how we were going to stay until Robinson was located. I explained to Justine and the girls what Scott had confirmed. There was no point in any more tests. I knew who killed Hayward, and who had abducted and arranged for the failed attempt on Scott's life: The same guy who had taken the girls for a boat ride.

Grace called as we were on our way out the door. I stopped in the lobby to answer.

"I can put out a BOLO on him and send a car by his house," she offered.

"If he's as jiggy as I think, he'll be listening to the scanner. We've got to keep this quiet or he's likely to bolt or try something stupid." It was the latter that worried me. "Sending a car by his house is a good idea." I gave her the names of the bars that the FWC hung out at, as well.

"We're going to head back to the island. I'll leave him to you," I told Grace.

The case was over for me. It was up to Miami-Dade to make the arrest.

A sense of relief washed over me as the pent-up emotions of the past week drained away. We left the lab and drove to the marina. The girls wanted to go with Justine in our new boat, both because of her, and of the speakers that lined the interior. As we idled into the river, I could hear the boom, boom, boom of the bass.

Passing the high-rise condos on Brickell Point, we turned to the south. Lining up the main span of the Rickenbacker Causeway with the bow, I was just about to push the throttles forward when I heard my phone. Glancing at the screen sitting face-up on the helm, I saw Susan McLeash's name, and realized there was one option for Robinson's location that I hadn't accounted for.

Stopping the boat, I picked up the phone, expecting Susan's voice.

"You've got something of mine, and I want it back." By calling from Susan's phone, Robinson didn't need to state the "or else."

"Slow down, there. There's more to this than just the bloody gauge."

"It's all hearsay. My service record speaks for itself. No jury is going to indict me."

"It's locked up in the evidence locker at the crime lab. Even if I wanted to play your game I couldn't get it."

"Get your wifey to help out, or you're going to be short a coworker."

I had no doubt he would follow through on that threat. "Let me talk to her."

There was a pause, then Susan came on the line.

"Kurt, he's freakin' crazy."

If Susan McLeash was calling someone crazy, I needed to pay attention. "Are you alright?"

"Yeah, for now. I don't trust him, though. I think he's on something."

That might explain his behavior. I was about to ask her where they were, hoping she might slip in a clue. When I heard Robinson's voice, I realized the phone must have been on speaker.

"Call me when you have it. You've got till midnight."

Susan's theory that he was under the influence explained a lot, but the knowledge made him harder to deal with. Robinson had made a mistake, though. In using Susan's phone, thanks to Martinez's paranoia, he had given me their location. Scrolling to her contact info, I saw the small map with a red dot. They were at her condo.

My phone dinged—a text from Allie asking if I was okay. Looking ahead, I saw the faint white stern light of our boat sitting on the water. I texted back I would be along shortly, and waited a second for them to disappear. With Robinson at Susan's, Adams Key was the safest place for my family. My phone dinged, showing a smiley face emoji. Girl-time trumps dad-time once again.

Able to put Justine and Allie's safety from my mind, I spun the wheel and headed back to Miami. Ducking into the river, I stopped the boat and called Grace. She met me a few minutes later at the marina. We were in her territory now, and whatever I did would reflect on her. Aside from that, Miami-Dade made a living out of dealing with crazies.

"The easiest thing to do would be to get a gauge and fake it," she said. That's why she'd made captain.

"At least for a decoy." I wasn't sure if I was going to endanger Susan's life with a ploy like that. Standing by her car, she called someone, asked whoever it was to do whatever I asked, and handed me the phone so I could describe the gauge. I would gladly donate some of my blood to make it look authentic, if it meant an end to this. She motioned to her car, but I declined.

"He's expecting me. Alone."

"I'll be right behind you. Find a strip center or something nearby, and we'll wait for backup there." She moved toward her car.

"Better keep it off the radio," I said.

She shot me a look and climbed into the driver's seat of her car. The reminder was one of those things I didn't want to say. You knew they knew, but with a life on the line, it was worth incurring her ire to confirm. There were a handful of Miami-Dade officers who wouldn't be either so smart, or so tactful.

With Grace behind me, we made our way south. Spotting a supermarket nearby, I pulled in and drove to a secluded part of the lot. Grace pulled up, and before we exited our vehicles, several other cars joined us. This was Grace's party now, and I stood back on the perimeter, catching "who's this guy?" glances from the other officers. Finally, a dark, armored truck rolled up

—SWAT had arrived. So long as we got Susan out alive, this was going to make her day.

With the briefing over, I stood on the outskirts of the group while we waited for the officer tasked with bringing the lobster gauge.

Feeling very much an outcast from the exclusive club, I checked my watch. It had been over an hour since Justine had taken off with the girls. When I called, she answered immediately, wanting to know why I had turned around. Being relegated to babysitter was not lost on her, and I could hear the disappointment in her voice when I explained what was happening. She understood that I was in a no-win situation, and fortunately, her attitude improved. I promised to keep her posted, and disconnected. Just as I did, a lone police car pulled in. Before the officer got out, the group converged on him.

There was no way to break through the dozen men in body armor, so I waited while Grace grabbed the new gauge and brought it to me. I picked it up, turning it in my hands. It wasn't a dead match, but Robinson was a desk jockey. Not handling the gauges every day during the eight-month season, he might not notice. It did strike me that it was new-looking.

"It'll probably pass, but we need to doctor it up." I dropped to my knees and rolled the gauge in the dirt of a landscape bed. It took a little of the sheen off, but it was still too clean. Pulling out my pocket knife, I opened the blade and prepared to puncture my finger. The flash of steel had the men surrounding me in seconds, and as I pressed the tip to my finger, I could sense their approval.

Grace held the gauge ready to catch the drops of blood. When I thought I'd donated enough, I took it from her and rubbed the blood all over it. The group pressed around me as I held the gauge up to the light. Ignoring them, I inspected it, deciding that without the original "weapon" for comparison, there was no way to tell the difference—unless Robinson had made some kind of distinguishing mark on it, and that was a possibility I couldn't cover.

I led the way to Susan's condo. As we approached, I could see headlights dropping off, first the marked cars, then the unmarked. The SWAT van stopped a block away. I pulled up in front of her condo, stopping in the space behind her truck. The plan was for me to wait here to allow the SWAT team and other officers who were on foot time to get in position

The condo was dark, but I could feel Robinson's eyes on me as I counted slowly to ten. Hoping it was long enough, I reached for my phone and pressed the icon beside Susan's name in my contacts. On the second ring he answered.

"Well, well, if it isn't the Lone Ranger," Robinson said.

Even if Susan hadn't tipped me off, I could tell by his voice he was under the influence, making me even more cautious. "I've got what you want. Why don't you let Susan go, and I'll bring it in."

"Not going to happen, Hunter. Bring it to the door."

I knew he was watching me, and I searched the dark windows looking for movement. He had at least enough sense to keep the house dark. Slowly I got out of the truck, fighting off my urge to look behind me for my backup, and with the gauge in hand, moved toward the front door. It cracked slightly as I approached, and when I reached the landing, a hand stuck out.

"Release her first. You have my word, I'll hand over the gauge once she's free."

The hand shot forward. Expecting him to grab the gauge, I yanked it back. That wasn't his intent and before I could react, Robinson had a hold of my shirt, and pulled me into the foyer. His action was so quick and unexpected that I went like a limp doll.

Once inside, the door slammed and I was pushed to the

floor. Blinking to adjust to the dim light, I saw the outline of Robinson standing over me. As my eyes acclimated to the darkness of the house, I could see the pistol in his hand.

"Let her go," I crawled to my knees, holding out the gauge as an offering.

He grabbed it from me and rolled it in his fingers. My night vision was fine-tuned now and I could see details. "Really, you think I'm that stupid? You've had plenty of time to get another one." He tossed it at my head.

I could see the tension in his arm extending to his index finger. It came to me in a flash: His plan had been to add Susan and me to his body count. Without us as witnesses, and if I was stupid enough to bring the real gauge with me, there would be no evidence against him. He already knew the real gauge wasn't enough evidence to indict him. It was Scott's fingerprints on the folds of the dry bag that placed Robinson in the bullseye.

His forearm twitched again. I had to act now. Lunging forward, I grabbed him around the ankles. It was a perfect tackle, but, coming from the floor, I was without any momentum or leverage. He kicked me aside, following my movement with the barrel of the gun. In slow motion, I saw his index finger tighten on the trigger. His finger twitched once. This gave me a fraction of a second to react, and I rolled to the side.

A shot fired, then another. My head was facing away, and it took me a second to realize I was still alive—and another that I wasn't hit. Sitting up, I saw Robinson's body on the floor with a dark liquid pooling around his head.

Behind him stood Susan McLeash with a gun in her hand.

EPILOGUE

STEVEN BECKER
A KURT HUNTER MYSTERY
BACKWATER FLATS

THERE'S SOMETHING ABOUT A NEAR-DEATH EXPERIENCE THAT leaves you both tired and wired. By the time I awoke the next day, sunlight streamed through the windows. Checking my watch on the nightstand, I realized it was past ten. Expecting to hear impatient voices coming from the living room, I leaned up on one elbow and listened. It was dead quiet. Without the urgency of entertaining Allie and Lana, I lay back down and let my mind drift, trying to sort out last night's events.

Having Susan McLeash save my life was an unexpected outcome, but I was glad for it. She was exonerated and would get the lion's share of the credit for taking down Robinson. I was the only one who knew the entire story, and it would stay with me. In the end, it was justice that I wanted, and it had been served.

I closed my eyes, but there was no going back to sleep. After the crime scene had wrapped up last night, I got a ride back to my boat and crossed the bay, arriving at Adams Key at four in the morning. The shooting had played over and over in my head until dawn broke, when I finally fell asleep.

Rising from bed, I realized I was still exhausted. A shower

helped, and in the kitchen I picked through the leftovers of breakfast and washed the dishes. With the girls and Justine gone, the couch beckoned and I was soon asleep again.

Excited voices coming up the stairs woke me, and before I could crack my eyes, Zero's tongue lashed my face. Fully awake now, I swung my legs to the floor.

"We got some yellowtails. Justine chummed them up. It was so much fun!" Allie said. Lana stood beside her, clearly as excited.

"Good afternoon, kemosabe." Justine relocated Zero, leaned over, and planted a kiss on my forehead. "They'll be down on the fish-cleaning table waiting for you."

"Can we go snorkeling again, Dad? Maybe to the reef this time?" Allie asked.

With the world back in alignment, I checked my watch. It was almost two. "I don't think we have enough time. We have dinner with Mariposa tonight. We're going to have to leave around five."

I could see the disappointment on their faces. "There's something we could do tomorrow, though, that might be fun and take care of your senior project."

She didn't look so enthused. "What's that?"

"I was thinking about setting up a pen in the lobster sanctuary where we could raise the shorts that the FWC confiscates."

"What a great idea!" She turned to Lana. "We can do it together." Standing in front of me, they started planning social media coverage and logistics. Their conversation took them back to Allie's room.

"That was a home run." My wife smiled at me.

"Not very original, though."

"No matter," Justine said, sitting down next to me. "You rocked it."

AFTERWORD

STEVEN BECKER
A KURT HUNTER MYSTERY
BACKWATER FLATS

The Florida Fish and Wildlife Conservation Commission (FWC) plays a valuable role in the preservation of Florida's natural resources. They are the heroes in many cases, doing an incredible job in managing our limited and often declining stocks in very difficult circumstances. To make matters worse, they are often caught in a political quagmire between special interest groups and the recreational anglers and hunters of the state. In no way was the portrayal of the FWC or its agents in Backwater Flats meant as a statement about, or an indictment, of them.

That said, the premise for the book came from their actions.

Around 1990, we lived in South Florida and often used Bayfront Park to launch our boat. One day when we were on our way in from a fishing and lobstering trip, we were stopped by a FWC boat, sitting where I portray it in the book. Of a half-dozen lobsters we'd caught, two were confiscated as shorts, something to this day I can't believe, as we always measured carefully. I remember thinking during the short trip across the canal that their gauges were fixed and they were stealing our lobsters.

That incident stayed with me for over twenty-five years. Now, maybe I can forget it!

Steven Becker - Tampa, Florida 2019

ABOUT THE AUTHOR

Always looking for a new location or adventure to write about, Steven Becker can usually be found on or near the water. He splits his time between Tampa and the Florida Keys - paddling, sailing, diving, fishing or exploring.

Find out more by visiting www.stevenbeckerauthor.com or contact me directly at booksbybecker@gmail.com.

facebook.com/stevenbecker.books
instagram.com/stevenbeckerauthor

**Get my starter library First Bite for Free!
when you sign up for my newsletter**

http://eepurl.com/-obDj

First Bite contains the first book in several of Steven Becker's series:

Get them now (http://eepurl.com/-obDj)

Mac Travis Adventures: The Wood's Series

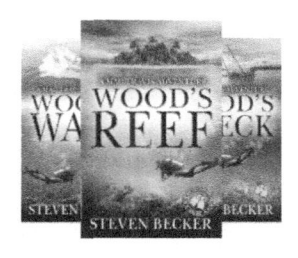

It's easy to become invisible in the Florida Keys. Mac Travis is laying low: Fishing, Diving and doing enough salvage work to pay his bills. Staying under the radar is another matter altogether. An action-packed thriller series featuring plenty of boating, SCUBA diving, fishing and flavored with a generous dose of Conch Republic counterculture.

Check Out The Series Here

★★★★★ *Becker is one of those, unfortunately too rare, writers who very obviously knows and can make you feel, even smell, the places he writes about. If you love the Keys, or if you just want to escape there for a few enjoyable hours, get any of the Mac Travis books - and a strong drink*

★★★★★ *This is a terrific series with outstanding details of Florida, especially the Keys. I can imagine myself riding alone with Mac through every turn. Whether it's out on a boat or on an island....I'm there*

Kurt Hunter Mysteries: The Backwater Series

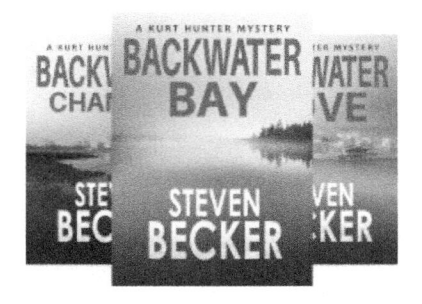

Biscayne Bay is a pristine wilderness on top of the Florida Keys. It is also a stones throw from Miami and an area notorious for smuggling. If there's nefarious activity in the park, special agent Kurt Hunter is sure to stumble across it as he patrols the backwaters of Miami.

Check it out the series here

★★★★★ *This series is one of my favorites. Steven Becker is a genius when it comes to weaving a plot and local color with great characters. It's like dessert, I eat it first*

★★★★★ *Great latest and greatest in the series or as a stand alone. I don't want to give up the plot. The characters are more "fleshed out" and have become "real." A truly believable story in and about Florida and Floridians.*

Tides of Fortune

What do you do when you're labeled a pirate in the nineteenth century Caribbean

Follow the adventures of young Captain Van Doren as he and his crew try to avoid the hangman's noose. With their uniques mix of skills, Nick and company roam the waters of the Caribbean looking for a safe haven to spend their wealth. But, the call "Sail on the horizon" often changes the best laid plans.

Check out the series here

★★★★★ *This is a great book for those who like me enjoy "factional" books. This is a book that has characters that actually existed and took place in a real place(s). So even though it isn't a true story, it certainly could be. Steven Becker is a terrific writer and it certainly shows in this book of action of piracy, treasure hunting,ship racing etc*

The Storm Series

Meet contract agents John and Mako Storm. The father and son duo are as incompatible as water and oil, but necessity often forces them to work together. This thriller series has plenty of international locations, action, and adventure.

Check out the series here

★★★★★ *Steven Becker's best book written to date. Great plot and very believable characters. The action is non-stop and the book is hard to put down. Enough plot twists exist for an exciting read. I highly recommend this great action thriller.*

★★★★★ *A thriller of mega proportions! Plenty of action on the high seas and in the Caribbean islands. The characters ran from high tech to divers to agents in the field. If you are looking for an adrenalin rush by all means get Steven Beckers new E Book*

The Will Service Series

If you can build it, sail it, dive it, and fish it—what's left. Will Service: carpenter, sailor, and fishing guide can do all that. But trouble seems to find him and it takes all his skill and more to extricate himself from it.

Check out the series here

★★★★★ *I am a sucker for anything that reminds me of the great John D. MacDonald and Travis McGee. I really enjoyed this book. I hope the new Will Service adventure is out soon, and I hope Will is living on a boat. It sounds as if he will be. I am now an official Will Service fan. Now, Steven Becker needs to ignore everything else and get to work on the next Will Service novel*

★★★★★ *If you like Cussler you will like Becker! A great read and an action packed thrill ride through the Florida Keys!*

Made in United States
Orlando, FL
10 September 2024